Donald P. Marsolais has recently retired from a teaching career after careers in banking and telecommunications. Prior to his 48 plus years in his three careers, he was an Eagle Scout and spent four years in the US Air Force. He began to write in high school for his own enjoyment and has never stopped. Don has a BA in English and an MPA. For the past 20 plus years, he has written Christmas stories for his family and friends. Now that he is retired; he is responding to family and friends by putting his stories in the book: *Twelve Days of Christmas Stories*. Don has also written *The Power of Positive Christian Teaching*.

Twelve Days of Christmas Stories is dedicated to my family and friends that continue to encourage me to write and share my Christmas short stories. I especially want to thank my wife, Barbara, who has never faltered in giving me her honest opinion.

Thanks to all!

Donald P. Marsolais

TWELVE DAYS OF CHRISTMAS STORIES

AUSTIN MACAULEY PUBLISHERS™

LONDON • CAMBRIDGE • NEW YORK • SHARJAH

Ordering Information
Quantity sales: Special discounts are available on quantity purchases by corporations, associations, and others. For details, contact the publisher at the address below.

Publisher's Cataloging-in-Publication data
Marsolais, Donald P.
Twelve Days of Christmas Stories

ISBN 9781638296263 (Paperback)
ISBN 9781638296270 (Hardback)
ISBN 9781638296287 (ePub e-book)

Library of Congress Control Number: 2021923203

www.austinmacauley.com/us

First Published 2021
Austin Macauley Publishers LLC
40 Wall Street, 33rd Floor, Suite 3302
New York, NY 10005
USA

mail-usa@austinmacauley.com
+1 (646) 5125767

Table of Contents

Introduction

Twelve Days of Christmas Stories is a compilation of stories that I have been writing for my family over the past 25–30 years. The stories in this book represent my best.

I have been writing for most of my adult life and it has only been since I have retired from teaching last year that I have focused on editing and publishing several works in progress. This is the second book to be published. My first was *The Power of Positive Christian Teaching*.

The stories in this book are fiction, but with an enormous amount of my own personal history used as the basis for writing the story. As such, many of the stories are family-based and can be read to your own family.

The intention of *Twelve Days of Christmas Stories* is to read one story a night with your own family for twelve nights leading up to Christmas. I recommend that you read it first and develop character voices then read it to your family on the second reading. My literature students always found my reading *The Adventures of Tom Sawyer* in character, or performance reading as I like to call it, a fun way to listen to a story. So did my family. I'm pretty sure that yours will, too.

My favorite story for creating your own character voices is *Mama's Night Out.* It deals with time travel, a Sam Spade type private investigator character, elves, and a secret held by a lady in red.

I believe that this book will enhance your family's Christmas season by adding a new tradition.

I hope that you enjoy reading *Twelve Days of Christmas Stories* as much as I enjoyed writing each story.

– Donald P. Marsolais

Day One
An Interesting Christmas

"Look, Mom! He's walking!" my sister yelled out.

Our little brother was just a year old and trying to keep pace with my sister and me. Jonas was born on Thanksgiving, 1946.

As far as I can remember, it wasn't much of a Thanksgiving except for Jonas coming. We were living with my grandparents in a small tenement flat that barely had enough room for them. Lolly and I shared the couch while Mom and Dad had the second bedroom along with Jonas. You're probably thinking, 'What kind of name is Lolly? What's that short for?' The best I can tell you is that her name is really Karen. I'm pretty sure that I started calling her Lolly around the time I started to talk. Had something to do with suckers.

Anyway, sleeping on the couch wasn't too bad except when Lolly wanted to have foot fights. We'd have our heads at either end of the couch and our feet would have to share the same space. When we were really tired, we'd just conk out and sleep was easy, but, when Mom or Dad put us to bed and we were still wide awake, we'd entertain ourselves by having foot fights.

The couch was in the parlor sitting on a carpet that had seen better days. There was a huge wing chair in the corner near a window that looked out on Main Street from our third-story flat. The parlor was just big enough for the couch, chair, and a stand-up lamp that gave off next to no light through the fringe on the lampshade. Just under the window was the radiator for heating. The walls were a dingy gray with family pictures and pictures of Jesus plastered all over them. There was a time that I thought Jesus was part of the family. Over time, however, I found out that I was right as we are all part of God's family.

"Kevin, come see what Jonas can do!" Lolly yelled. I came into the parlor from the kitchen just in time to see baby Jonas take two steps then plop right down on his butt. He was giggling and chasing after a ball that Lolly had given him for his birthday. He was an energetic child and, now that he could almost walk, wanted to go everywhere.

It was Christmas break from school and Lolly got to take care of me and Jonas while Mom and Dad were at work. Grandma and Grandpa had gone to visit relatives for a few days so we were all alone in the flat. Lolly was twelve and I was ten so we really didn't need sitters. At least that's what we thought.

With only two days left before Christmas, the house looked as it always did. There were no decorations up, no tree, no wreath for the door, nothing. It was looking like there would be no Christmas. On that day, Lolly woke up at the same time as Mom and Dad. They left for work around 7:00. As soon as they were gone, she jumped out of bed, brushed her teeth, put cold water on her face, and brushed her golden hair. She looked into the mirror at her deep blue eyes and simply said, "We can do this."

I heard her rummaging around in the little cupboard in the back of the kitchen, but I was too tired to get up and see what was going on. I nodded off to sleep and didn't wake up until Lolly came into the parlor.

I rubbed my eyes and said, "What are you doing? Where's Jonas?"

"Jonas is fine. I gave him his bottle, fed him some warm cereal, and put him down for his morning nap."

"Nap? What time is it anyway?" I asked. The sun was peeking through a cloud cover that promised snow. Lolly raised the shade in the parlor and let the gray from the outside into the inside.

"That's what we need. Now I can see what we're doing," she said.

I rubbed my eyes again trying to get adjusted to the light and said, "What time is it?"

"Time to get up, sleepy head. I've got everything set up and ready to go, but I need your help."

I wasn't quite awake yet and answered, "My help? What are you doing? What are you getting us into?" I looked around the parlor for a clue. Nothing.

"Just get up. You'll see," Lolly said with authority.

I got up, went to the bathroom, did my business, and rushed out to see what it was that she was getting us into. I didn't even take time to brush my teeth or comb my hair. "Lolly? Where are you?"

"Come into the kitchen," she replied.

As I made my way from the bathroom to the kitchen, I could see what she was talking about. The kitchen was all decorated with garland and tinsel. "Where did you get all that?" I asked.

"It was in the pantry cupboard. I remembered it from last year when we helped Grandpa take down the decorations."

I started to rummage through the boxes of decorations. One box had Christmas ornaments for a tree and the other had decorations for the rest of the house.

"So, you need my help to do what? It seems like you have it pretty well in hand."

"It may look that way, but there is one big thing that I can't do by myself. Get out of your PJs and I'll tell you what we need to do."

Just then, Jonas woke up. Lolly went into the bedroom, changed him, put some clothes on him, and brought him out to the kitchen.

By the time I got back into the kitchen, Lolly was fixing Jonas a mid-morning bottle. "So, what do you need my help with?" I asked again.

"Let me finish feeding Jonas then I'll tell you. In the meantime, why don't you go through that box of ornaments and make sure that they have hooks so that we can put them on the tree," she said.

"What tree?" I blurted. I was a little slow at ten, but it didn't take me long to figure out why Lolly needed my help.

"Oh, we're getting a Christmas tree," Lolly said.

"Are Mom and Dad bringing it home with them?" I asked.

"Not exactly," she said. "We're going out to get one and surprise them when they get home. Are you in?"

"Well, yeah, but did they give you money to buy a tree? Do Mom and Dad even know about this?" I was starting to see several flaws in the plan.

"No, I don't have any money. We're going to cut one down in the park across the street," Lolly casually said.

"What? Are you insane? That has to be against the law. It's a park for crying out loud!" I screamed.

My response was so loud that Jonas started crying as he lay in his crib that Lolly had wheeled out of the bedroom. Poor Jonas. He dropped his bottle and let out a screech louder than the teakettle's whistle.

"Now see what you've done?" Lolly said with some anger in her voice. "Go finish sorting the ornaments while I quiet him down."

Jonas was a good baby, but he could be quite obnoxious when he started in on one of his crying jags. This was one of those times. I had scared him and he wasn't about to be consoled until he wore himself out. He cried and cried and cried as Lolly rocked him in Grandma's rocker. Fifteen minutes later, he was just sobbing and another fifteen minutes after that, he was asleep in Lolly's arms. I remember thinking how good a mom she would make. Time would prove that to be a true thought.

Before she got up from the rocker, she had me wheel his crib back into the bedroom. She followed me and carefully placed him in the crib. He would sleep for a few hours before he woke up hungry.

"You have so much patience with him," I said.

"It's no big thing. What other option is there? I could get all upset as he was. How would that help?"

She was right, of course. "I just mean, you are so natural with him. I would have to force myself to not be bothered by all that screeching." That's true to this day. I still cringe whenever I hear a baby screech. It doesn't even have to be one of my own grandchildren. It doesn't matter. A kid screeches and I'm looking for a way out. But enough of that. Back to the Christmas of 1947.

"Let's get back to this hair-brained idea you have of going across the street and cutting down a tree. Never mind that it's a park, just how do you propose to do that in broad daylight?" I was being a little sarcastic, but plainly I thought it was a bad idea. "And, what do you think Mom and Dad are going to say when you tell them you cut down a tree from the park?"

By the look on her face, it was clear that she hadn't thought of that. She lowered her head a little and simply said, "I never really thought of that. It's just that I wanted to surprise them with a decorated house and tree. They've done so much for us." She started to cry.

"Don't cry. We'll think of something. Let's make some lunch and talk it over. You make some sandwiches and I'll pour the milk."

Lolly got out the bologna link and carved off two slices; one for her and one for me. The bread had been baked just yesterday and was still fresh. Four slices with a little mustard and our sandwiches were ready to go. We talked as we ate. By the time we were finished, we had a plan.

"I'll wash the dishes and you get Jonas ready to go," I said.

"We can't go yet. I have to feed him again."

"There's always something with that little guy. What do you think of staying here with him and I'll get the tree on my own. I'm pretty sure I can handle it."

"I don't know," she said. "Are you sure you can get there and back without any problem?" She was more concerned about me getting there and back rather than if I could do what needed to be done to get a tree. I felt good that she trusted me to be able to get a tree without her.

"It won't be a problem. Plants is only a half mile away. Mom and Dad have an account there. I know Mr. Plant. I'm sure he'll give me a tree if I tell him to put it on our account. No problem. I'll be back in no time at all." I was sure this would be a better option than cutting down a park tree.

"Okay, but you better hurry. Those storm clouds don't look like they'll wait forever before it starts to snow."

I got my galoshes, coat, hat, and mittens on then made my way to the store. It only took me about fifteen minutes to get there, but in that time, it had already started to snow. I talked with Mr. Plant and, not only did he put the tree on our account, he gave me a $1.00 discount because it was so close to Christmas and he didn't want to have to deal with leftover trees on Christmas Eve.

There wasn't much left to choose from, but I did take the one that I thought would fit best in the tenement. "Thank you, Mr. Plant," I shouted and waved to him as he stood in the door of his store.

"Kevin, do you want a ride? The snow is coming down pretty hard now," he yelled as I continued to walk.

"No, thanks. It's not that far." I waved again and trudged off into the falling snow dragging the tree behind me. I must have gone only a block before the clouds opened up as they had never done before in my ten years of life. I was in a total white-out. I stopped and thought about going back to the store, but decided to continue on. Two blocks later, I didn't know where I was. I didn't even know if I was on my street or somewhere else. I decided to do what Dad had always told us kids to do if we ever got lost – just stay put and someone would find us.

My coat, hat, galoshes, and mittens were warm enough for a short trip, but the biting cold was starting to come through them and I began to shiver. I huddled in the tree that was collecting snow as fast as I could shake it free. I must have been there ten minutes when I heard a car's wheels crunching in the snow. Then I saw them; two headlights heading right for me. It must have been because I was half-frozen, but I couldn't move as fast as I needed to. I jumped out of the road just as the car skidded to a stop right where I had been sitting.

A man got out of the car. "Are you alright, son? I almost didn't see you. Where are you going?" He didn't even wait for me to answer. "Let me take you home."

Mom and Dad had always taught us to not talk to strangers, but this was an emergency and I figured that it would be okay just this once. "That would be swell, mister," I said.

"Here, let me put that tree in the backseat. You get in the front."

I did as I was told and huddled shivering in the front seat as the man put the tree in the back. He opened the door and got in. "So, what's your name and where do you live and why are you out in a snowstorm?"

Three questions all at the same time. "My name is Kevin and I live at 691 Belmont Street and I was bringing a tree home to my family," I answered.

"Belmont? Do you know where you are? Belmont is five blocks the other way. Okay, let's get you home."

"That would be great, sir. I really do appreciate it. I was trying to get home before my parents came home from work. We wanted to surprise them by decorating our flat for Christmas." Right after saying this, I wondered if I had said too much.

"No problem, Kevin. I'll get you home and help you get that tree into your flat also."

It took us only a few minutes to get to my place. He parked the car and got the tree out of the backseat. I closed the door for him and led him up to the third floor.

"Lolly! Lolly! Are you here?" I yelled as I entered the door.

Lolly came out of the bedroom with Jonas all bundled up. She had her winter coat and hat on with a scarf wound tightly around her neck. She had mittens on her hands.

"Where have you been? I was worried about you. I called Mr. Plant and he told me that you left almost an hour ago."

"It's a long story, but Mr. uhhh. I didn't get your name."

"It's Klaus, Klaus Noel. Pleased to meet you, young lady. Looks like you are going somewhere. Can I drop you any place?" he said in a foreign accent that sounded like German.

"No, I was just going to look for my brother, but he's here now." She started to unwind her scarf and take off her mittens. She undressed Jonas and put him back in his crib while I got out of my wet clothes.

"Can I get you some cocoa, Mr. Noel?" Lolly offered.

"No, no, I'm fine. I need to be off. I just wanted to make sure that you kids were alright. When do your parents get home?"

I looked at the clock on the kitchen wall. It was nearly 5:00. "Mom and Dad should be home any time," I answered. It had been a long day.

"Alright, I'll take off then. You kids have a Merry Christmas," Mr. Noel said as he went out the door.

Mom and Dad got home a little later than usual because of the heavy snow. Needless to say, they were surprised to see all the decorations when they got home.

"How did you do all this?" Mom asked.

"It was Lolly," I answered. "She had this great idea to surprise you when you got home tonight. Look!" I pointed to the corner in the parlor. "There's even a tree that we can decorate tonight."

"You have been very busy children," Dad said. "How did you get the tree? I hope you didn't cut one down in the park?"

Lolly and I just looked at each other and started to laugh and then, in unison, we said, "If you only knew." We laughed some more.

Day Two
Angels All Around Us

Have you ever seen an angel? I mean a real angel? Not the kind you see in pictures with wings and all that stuff, but a real angel. I know what you're thinking. How would I know an angel if I did see one? It's easy. It's simply an ordinary person doing extraordinary things to help an individual, a family, a community, a country, the world.

I know, I know! You're thinking that, if that's the description of angels, you must be seeing them every day and not even know it. That's pretty much true, but you can recognize them by their behavior. Watch for the person that is willing to help others without being prompted. That person is an angel to the person they're helping.

I try to be an angel at least once a day. It's an amazing feeling to help others. God gave us angels the spirit to be emotional and respond with emotion to our brothers and sisters. On this day before Christmas Eve, let me tell you about my first encounter with a guardian angel.

I was twelve almost thirteen I think, and I'd heard about guardian angels, but I never thought that I'd see one. I thought that angels were simply spirits God sent to watch over us. I didn't know at the time that they were living, breathing beings.

Anyway, at twelve, I was just beginning to feel more responsible for myself. I didn't want to have to ask permission from Mom and Dad to do everything, so I started making my own decisions – some of them good and some not so good. Each time I did something I knew was a little wrong, I'd feel guilty, but continue to do it because I'd be seen as a 'chicken' by my friends if I didn't go along with them. I later would identify this behavior as peer pressure.

At my age, having friends to share my life with was what helped to make me responsible (or so I thought). I had been lying to my mother for a few months. At first, I felt bad about it, but the more I lied, the easier it became to lie again. It was like an addiction. I just told whatever story I thought of to get out of the house or explain away some poor behavior.

My Mom's not dumb. She saw what was happening, but thought that I was just having growing pains. She thought that I would grow out of it. In a way, she was right. I did grow out of it, just not in the way she was thinking. Let me tell you how all this ties into meeting my first guardian angel.

It was late November in 1955 and my best friend, Marco, and I would spend almost every afternoon walking downtown to Jay's Music to listen to the new records that were climbing the charts. We both liked rock and roll and, when we got our allowances, would buy 45s to play on our record players.

Well, here we were in late November getting ready for winter. The air had been getting colder and colder as the days went by. Soon, we would have the first snow of the season and our afternoon strolls would end. We'd be cooped up in the house until the spring thaws came.

I remember it well. It was a Thursday and before going into Jay's we stopped in at the local drug store to buy some candy. Marco had just enough money to buy the new Elvis Presley record so he asked me if he could borrow a quarter to get some candy. I also had just enough to get my own candy and a record, so I told him, "I don't have any extra." I selected my candy and went to the counter to pay for it. Marco made his way out of the store and slipped into the record shop next door.

Standing behind the counter was a girl I recognized. It was Anne from the high school. I knew her because her sister, Jane, was in my class and Anne would come to pick her up from school every once in a while.

"Hi, I know you. Your sister is Jane in 7th grade over at Parker Elementary, right?"

"That's right. How did you know?"

"I'm in Jane's class and I've seen you picking her up from school."

"What's your name?" she asked with a smile on her face.

This blonde-haired, blue-eyed, junior had me tongue-tied. Everyone called me Donny, but my real name is Donald. I couldn't tell her my name was Donny. That would be too juvenile and Donald was too formal so I split the difference and simply said, "Uh, I'm Don." I spoke it just as though I was the pimply, overweight, low self-esteem kid that I was.

"Well, nice to meet you, Don. I hope my sister doesn't cause you too much trouble. She's a pretty good kid at home, but you know how you kids are when you're away from your parents."

"No, she's great. We're partners in science class. She's really smart. I'm lucky to be her partner," I said trying to sound intelligent.

"Is that going to be all?" she asked. I laid the candy bar I had in my hand on the counter. I was so nervous at meeting Anne that I had squashed the Milky Way with the heat of my hand.

"Yes, that's it." I reached into my pocket for the quarter that I had brought for the candy when she asked me something that turned my blood ice cold.

"Are you paying for your friend who left the store with a Baby Ruth? I would hate to turn him in as a thief for such a small amount."

Now she knew who I was and knew that she could get to Marco through me. I was in a real pickle. Do I challenge her or pay her? Would Marco really steal a candy bar or was Anne trying to get an easy quarter out of me? I decided that paying for the Baby Ruth was a better idea than telling Anne I thought that she must be mistaken.

"Sure, sure. Marco must have been so excited to get the new Elvis record that he forgot to pay for the candy bar." I took out the dollar bill that I had for my record and handed it over to Anne.

"Here you are," and she handed me my $.75 change. "Maybe I'll see you again," she added.

"You might. Say hi to Jane for me." That was it. I walked out of the store and went straight into the record store. There was Marco looking through the stacks of 45 rpm records eating the Baby Ruth.

"What were you thinking, stealing that candy bar? Did you think that you'd get away with that?"

Marco made a face as though I had just accused him of stealing and I had. "What's the big deal? It's only a $.25 candy bar. I got away with it, didn't I?"

"No, you didn't. She saw you take it and asked if I was going to pay for you. Of course, I said yes and gave up the quarter. Now I don't have enough for the Elvis record. How 'bout giving me the quarter I paid for the candy?" I said.

Marco walked down the aisle a little ways with me following him. "I didn't ask you to pay for it," Marco spouted. "I'm getting the Presley. What you do with your money is your business, not mine."

"Seriously, you aren't going to pay me back for covering for you?"

Marco responded with an attitude in his voice, "Seriously, stop being a pain in the butt. I told you I'm not going to give you the quarter. Maybe if you don't have enough money for a record, you should go home or be bold enough to just take what you want."

"I can't believe that you're suggesting that I steal from the record store. Marco, I thought I knew you, but what I'm seeing today has shaken my trust in you."

"Don't give me that trust crap. If you don't like what you see, go home and leave me alone." He walked up the aisle, paid for his record, and left the store.

I felt terrible. Not only did I have to cover for my best friend, but now my best friend pretty much told me to get lost. In a way, I was glad that he was in a different 7th grade than me. Now I didn't have to go out of my way to get together with him for our afternoon strolls. I left Jay's without the Presley.

The next day, as I was walking down the corridor, I saw Marco being hauled into the vice principal's office. The VP was also the dean of discipline. *What could this be about,* I thought.

I walked into the office with some lame excuse to speak to the secretary, Miss Johnson. "I just saw my friend Marco go into Mr. Burgess's office. Do you know if he'll be in there long? We're supposed to walk home together."

Miss Johnson hesitated then said, "My guess is that his parents will be picking him up today. Smoking, you know."

I couldn't believe my ears. What was happening to my best friend? It sounded like he was trying to sabotage his life that hadn't really even begun yet.

"Thanks. I guess I'll walk home alone. See ya, Miss Johnson."

"Bye, Donny." Because of Anne, I now hated that name.

When I got home, I went straight to my room and did my homework. Don't ask me why. I usually put homework off to the end of the night. It took me about an hour and when I had finished, I went downstairs to get a glass of water.

"Donny, can you help me set the table, please? Your father will be home in a little bit and I want to eat early because tonight's Bowling Night. We have to leave by 5:30."

Oh, no! Bowling Night meant that old Mrs. Jackson would be over to 'babysit' me. She was absolutely no fun. I'm sure that she was only in her 50s or 60s, but she acted like she was in her 80s. All she wanted to do was watch TV and knit. She never wanted to play any games.

"Did you finish your homework?" my mom asked. "We're trying out a new babysitter for you tonight. Mrs. Jackson wasn't available. I'll want you to tell me how you like Anne when we get home."

Could it be? Was my babysitter, Anne, going to be candy counter Anne? I couldn't tell if that was going to be good or bad. Did I really want her to babysit me? What would she think of me?

Just as I finished setting the table, Dad walked in. "Hi, son. What's new at school today?" He seriously wanted to know. *Should I tell him about Marco's behavior change or not?* I decided to check in with Dad and see what he thought.

"Dad, what would you do if you thought that a friend was in trouble?" He had already sat down in his overstuffed chair and had just opened the paper to the Sports Section.

"Hm. What did you say? Something about being in trouble. You in trouble?" He dropped the paper into his lap still opened to the Sports Section. "What's this all about?"

"No, Dad. Not me. Marco, my friend from school, is having some trouble with making good decisions. Should I talk to him or his parents?" I really needed his advice, but all I got was referred to my mother.

I walked into the kitchen to the smell of pot roast vegetables and gravy being ladled out of the roasting pan and into a bowl. The roast had already been placed on a platter. It was perfectly done and waiting to be carved. Dinner was on the table so I decided to wait to ask Mom what I should do.

"Honey, can you carve the roast, please?" Mom yelled to Dad.

"I'll be right in. Are we still going bowling tonight?" he asked.

"Yes, Anne will be here in a half hour to sit with Donny. She's new, but she comes highly recommended by the girls in my book club. She's a junior over at the high school."

Dad came into the kitchen, got out the carving knife and fork, and proceeded to expertly slice the roast. As soon as the knife slid into the meat, the juices ran down and into the platter leaving the best smell in the air. I was hungry in an instant.

"Donny, can you get yourself a glass of milk and pour a cup of coffee for me and your father?" That wasn't new. I always poured the coffee and got my own milk. Mom always had a pot of coffee brewing on the stove.

Dad finished carving the roast, Mom placed the vegetables and gravy on the table, and I got the bread and butter after placing the coffee and milk at each of our places. We all sat down, held hands, and said Grace. We always thanked God for our meals and each other. I can't say that we were "holy-holies," but we believed in a power greater than ourselves and we called him God.

The meal was so good that no one spoke. We just ate until Dad asked me to get some more coffee for him and Mom.

She said, "You might want to refill your milk glass. I baked an apple pie today." I didn't have to be asked twice.

As I got the coffee and milk, Mom got up, opened the fridge, and took out the pie. She sliced three pieces and put them on little plates. Just as I was about to take my first bite, the doorbell rang.

"I'll get it," I said as I jumped out of my chair and made my way to the door. I knew that it had to be Anne. I opened the door and there she was – my future wife. Silly of me to think that, but I fancied myself already in love with her. Don't ask me why. My guess is hormones.

"Hi, Anne. Remember me?" I stuttered.

"Yeah, the kid from the candy store that goes to school with my sister. How's that science project coming along?"

I couldn't believe that she remembered that Jane and I were partners in science class. "We're doing pretty good. Our project is going to be part of the Science Fair just before the Christmas break in a week. Did she tell you what we are doing?" I asked.

We walked into the living room heading into the kitchen as she said, "Something about thrust, I think."

"Yeah, I'll tell you all about it later if you're interested. Do you want some pie? My mom baked it this morning."

"I'd love some. Hello, Mr. and Mrs. Ambrose. I'm Anne Haskins. I don't know if Don told you or not, but my sister and he are in the same class and are working on a science project together for the Science Fair next week."

As she was talking, I went to get another plate for the pie and turned around just as she said "Don." The expression on my parents' faces was priceless. I don't think that they had ever heard anyone call me Don.

"That's interesting, dear," my mom said. "What is your favorite subject in school?"

"I really like English. I have a great teacher who allows us to spread our wings with the short story writing we are working on. I think I want to be an author when I get out of college."

"Do you know where you want to go after high school? There are some great schools nearby."

Anne seemed to squirm a little before answering. "I'm not sure that I want to go right to college. I was thinking of taking a year off, living life, and getting experiences that I can use for my writing. Of course, that may all change. My parents aren't too keen on that path for me."

"I can see why they would have some reservations with that plan. It's not exactly what I would choose for my daughter if I had one," Dad said.

Mom saw where this was going and simply said, "Dear, look at the time. We'll be late." That was all she had to say and Dad got up, went upstairs, changed into his bowling shirt, and came down with his bowling bag in hand. Mom was next, but she had to clean off the table and do the dishes.

"Why don't you let Don and I do those dishes, Mrs. Ambrose?" Anne turned to me and said, "I'll wash and you dry. You okay with that, Don?"

All I could think of to say was, "Fine, I like to dry." I lied. I hate to dry.

Mom gave Anne all the particulars of where the emergency phone numbers were and also the phone number to the bowling alley.

"I know that it's Friday, but please don't keep him up too late. Maybe 10:00 would be a good bed time. We'll be home around 11:00."

"No problem, Mrs. Ambrose. Ten o'clock it is."

We spent the first couple of hours just getting to know each other and playing some kid board games that were left over from my childhood. Finally, I decided to up the ante with this beauty.

"How would you like me to make a fire in the fireplace? I do it all the time." I could tell that Anne wasn't too sure about that.

"I don't think that would be a good idea, Don," she said with some stress in her voice. "I'm pretty sure that your parents would not want that. I'm gonna say no. Maybe some other time when you have cleared it with your parents."

I didn't want to push it so I said, "No problem. Like you said, maybe some other time."

We sat back on the couch after playing the board games on the kitchen table. "Anne, can I ask you something?"

"Sure, what do you want to know?"

"Well, I have this friend who seems to be getting into a lot of trouble lately. What can I do to help him straighten himself out?" I wasn't sure that she would have any answers, but it was worth a try.

"I had a friend like that in my freshman year. We were good friends until she got in with the wrong crowd. She began by lying to her parents about where she was going. She started smoking and drinking. She wanted me to join her and her new girlfriends, but I knew that I didn't want that lifestyle for myself so I simply said no."

"What happened next?" I asked.

"Just what you'd expect. She dumped me for the new crowd. At first, I was sad, but eventually, I realized that my choice was good for me. I was pretty sure that Lisa's choice wasn't good for her, but there was no telling her that. As we started our sophomore year, she and I no longer spoke. She just didn't want anything to do with me anymore. I respected her choice until one day it was apparent that she was drunk at school."

"What did you do?"

"I called her out on it at lunch. We had a big row. I was trying to help her get away from her behavior, but she wouldn't hear of it. Her new friends came over to see what was going on. As you would expect, they took her side and physically pushed me away from her. I knew that I was beaten so I just left."

"That was pretty courageous of you. What did you do next?"

"The only thing I could do. I went to her parents and told them what I had been seeing. They were nice enough, but seemed to not care. They thanked me for coming over, but pretty much told me to butt out of their affairs. By this time, I was scared for Lisa. I knew that I had to do more to get her to change back to the warm-hearted, generous person I knew as a freshman."

When I asked my question, I never expected so much information. The story Anne was telling had a lot of good points that I would be willing to try with Marco. "Did you ever get Lisa away from that crowd and back to her old self?"

Anne began to sob. "Give me a minute, please. Are there any tissues?"

I got some from the bathroom and gave them to her. She had stopped sobbing, but her eyes were red and her cheeks wet. She dabbed at her eyes and blew her nose. "Is there anything I can do to help?" I asked.

"No, I'm fine." She blew her nose again, then continued with the story. "Since I was sure that Lisa's parents weren't going to do anything, I went to the vice principal and let her know what was going on. To her credit, she listened to my concerns and said that she would look into it. I wasn't sure if 'looking into it' would be enough. The next thing I know, I'm being dragged into the principal's office for stalking Lisa. Mrs. Henderson had information from Lisa's friends and her parents saying that I was trying to force Lisa to be my friend again."

"What happened then?"

"I was at the end of my rope, but I wasn't going to give up. There was going to be a homecoming party at one of the football players' house. His parents were on vacation and he had the house all to himself. I wasn't invited, because my reputation of being a 'goody-goody' just didn't fit in with what may happen at the party. I knew that Lisa and her friends were going, so I invited myself."

"Wasn't that risky? I mean, you already weren't welcome. What did you think that Lisa and her friends would do when they saw you there?"

"I didn't care. I just knew that something bad was going to happen if I didn't do something. As soon as I walked through the door, it was apparent that this party was already out of control. People were smoking and drinking and who knows what else. I wandered through the house with a beer in my hand just to look like I belonged. Then I saw Lisa and her crowd. They were playing a drinking game. Some of her friends were already passed out on a couch."

"Let me get this straight. There was a huge party, there were no adults present, and beer and liquor was there. If I saw that, I would get the heck out of there. What did you do?"

Anne began sobbing again. "The only thing I could do. I went next door and called the cops."

"Wow! That took guts. What happened?"

Within five minutes, two squad cars rolled up. Two police officers entered the open door, took one look around, and blew a whistle.

"'Who's in charge here? Who owns this house?'" they demanded.

"As soon as they opened their mouths, people started pouring out of the back door, leaving all their drinks on the grass, in the pool, and all over the house. The cops roamed the house looking to see who was still there. They found Lisa and her two friends passed out. I introduced myself to the officers and told them that I was the one who called about the party. They thanked me and told me that the three girls would be brought to the hospital then go to jail because of their underage drinking.

"'You look pretty sober. Didn't you drink?' they asked.

"'No, officer. I came to the party to keep an eye on my friend. I was just about to drive her home when you arrived. Is there any way that I can just take Lisa home and eliminate her going to jail?'

"'I don't know about that. Your friend should have to pay some consequences for her bad choices. The law says that jail is what she needs to answer for her crime.'

"'Please, Officer. I promise that she won't do anything like this again. It was her first time.'

"'Miss, I don't usually give breaks to minors because you have to learn young that you just can't do what you want without having to pay for it, but I'm going to make an exception in this case. You take your friend home and we'll forget about this,'" he said.

"I splashed some cold water on Lisa's face, got her on her feet, and into the car. By the time I got her home, my home, she had thrown up twice outside of the car, thankfully. I put her to bed and stayed up all night with her. In the morning, she asked what had happened and I told her."

"What was her response?"

"She broke down in tears and apologized for her rotten behavior, swearing that she would never do that again. She asked for my forgiveness and I gave it to her. After that, I gave her a ride to her home. We left as friends once again."

"So, if I understand your story, I should do whatever it takes to make sure that Marco is in a good place and not hanging out with a bad bunch. Does that sound about right?"

"Pretty much right on," she said.

"It seems to me that you were Lisa's guardian angel that night."

"I guess you could say that. Over the next two weeks leading up to Christmas, we were friends again. We even went to Midnight Mass together. Guess what the sermon was about?"

Even though I went to Midnight Mass, I couldn't for the life of me remember the sermon. "I can't remember exactly, but my guess is that it had something to do with the birth of Jesus. Am I right?"

"Sort of. The priest spoke of the birth of Christ and also spoke of how God's angels announced his birth to the surrounding shepherds. He especially spoke of how guardian angels have been sent by God to watch over us and, if we take care of each other, we become those guardian angels."

Just as Anne finished the story, my parents came home. "Well, not in bed I see," my mother quipped.

"Mom, it's not Anne's fault. I had a problem that she helped me with. I'm tired. I'll talk to you in the morning. Good night, Anne, and thanks." I kissed both my mom and dad and went up to bed.

"What was that all about?" My dad asked Anne as he handed her the agreed upon payment, plus a tip.

"Oh, nothing much. Don just wanted to know about angels. Good night."

Day Three
Christmas Memories

So, I knew that last Christmas would be difficult, but I never believed that out of our family's sadness could come such joy. Here's how I remember it.

Last year, during the 4th of July weekend, both of my parents were killed in a car crash near Lake Tahoe. They were run off the road by an out-of-control big rig. It forced them through a guardrail and they tumbled over 500 feet to the river at the bottom. The Highway Patrol said that most likely they were dead before they hit the bottom.

My wife and I had just finished with our 4th of July afternoon barbecue and the kids were in the pool as Janie and I lounged under the gazebo with our neighbors. It was hot, but not sweltering. In fact, at 84 degrees, it was one of the cooler 4th of Julys in recent years.

The twins, Nancy and Norman, now twelve, were having a good time with some neighbor kids. They would have liked their cousins to be there, but it was not to be. It had been several years since our entire family had gotten together for anything.

My brother, Jake, and his wife, Natalie, live in Eureka, California, with their three kids; James, Jackie, and Justin.

At five, Jackie is the youngest of the cousins. The boys are twelve and thirteen. My sister, LuLu, her husband, Mike, and their two kids, Zane and Zack, live in smog city, Los Angeles. The boys are around ten and twelve.

As we relaxed with our neighbors, munched on chips and such, drank a few beers, and took pictures of the kids having fun, the phone rang. Normally, I'd just let it ring because of the nuisance calls we constantly receive from sales people, but this time I ran inside to answer it thinking that it may be some of the family calling. It wasn't.

"Mr. Simmons, this is Sergeant MacClain of the California Highway Patrol."

"What can I do for you, Sergeant?"

"Are your parents Kate and Jack Simmons?"

"Yes, why do you ask?" I had a bad feeling about this.

"Mr. Simmons, I have some bad news for you. At 3:30 this afternoon, a run-away-truck crossed over the center line on Highway 50 just outside of Lake Tahoe and collided with your parents' car."

"Oh, my God! Are they alright? Are they hurt?" I ran my sentences together in haste hoping to get a positive reply that they were alright.

"I'm sorry to have to inform you that both your mother and father were killed in the accident. Their car ran through the guardrail over the embankment and plummeted over 500 feet to the bottom near the river. I'm sorry. Do you have someone with you right now? Do we need to send someone out to assist you?"

I just stood there stunned. I didn't know what to say.

"Mr. Simmons? Are you there?" the Sergeant asked obviously interested in my well-being.

"I–I'm here," I stuttered. "I have people here. What happens next?" I asked.

"We'll be transporting their bodies to a mortuary of your choosing. Do you know where that will be?"

Luckily, Mom and Dad had selected a mortuary and grave site already so all I had to do was contact them and they would take care of everything.

"Yes, can you contact Pride Mortuary in Folsom? My parents have an arrangement with them. I'll call them in the morning."

"We can do that. Your parents should be there late tomorrow. The car was totaled and will be recovered within the next week. It will be deposited in the Lake Tahoe Salvage Yard. You should get in touch with their insurance carrier to let them know of the accident and the disposition of the vehicle. Is there anything else I can do for you, Mr. Simmons?"

After validating that I had the information correct, I said good-bye and hung up the phone. I took a deep breath and sat down at the kitchen table to get my bearings. How was I going to tell Janie and the kids? Being the eldest son, I got the call so now it was on me to call Jake and LuLu. I wasn't sure that I was up for that task. I needed Janie.

I poked my head out of the slider and called to her. "Honey, can you come in here for a minute, please?" I think she sensed that something was wrong because she got right out of her chair and came in. Usually, she would have asked me what I wanted.

"What is it, Tom? Do you need help finding something?"

I just stared at her. "Janie, take a seat. I have some bad news."

She sat and said, "Tell me. What is it?"

As I started to tell her, I completely broke down and couldn't talk. I went into uncontrollable sobs. Janie came to me, hugged me, and tried to soothe me.

"Honey, what is it? Tell me so I can help you. Is it one of your parents? Your mom? Your dad?" She kissed me on the cheek. "It'll be okay. We can get through whatever it is. Please tell me."

As she stroked my head, I began to get a hold of myself and I stopped sobbing. "It's unbelievable." Through sniffles, I finished telling her what happened. "Mom and Dad are dead. There was an accident on Highway 50 just outside of Tahoe. They're both gone." I started crying again. What was I going to do? My parents were my best friends. Then I remembered that I had to call Jake and LuLu.

"Honey, can you tell the kids while I call my brother and sister?" She agreed and went into the backyard, told the neighbors what had happened, told them that she'd let them know when there were arrangements, and asked if they wouldn't mind calling it a party. They all understood, gave Janie their condolences, and left.

Janie told the kids and I told Jake and LuLu. As you might expect, all of them were basket cases when they got the news. The next few days were a whirlwind of activities. I called my boss and asked for a week off to take care of everything. She was very understanding and gave me one week bereavement leave and extended me more time if I needed it.

Janie doesn't work so she took on the responsibility of the kids. She did a great job explaining that Grandma and Grandpa weren't going to be around anymore. While the kids were sad, our Christian faith helped them understand that they were in a better place.

The day of the funeral came and relatives from all over the country came in to pay their respects. It was the first time in two years that I had seen my brother and sister. We pledged to each other that we would get together again under different circumstances.

Mom and Dad were pillars of St. John's parish. So, it was not a surprise that it was standing room only for their funeral. It was beautiful with flowers on either side of the altar remembering my parents both as a couple and as individuals. Both Janie and I coordinated the day's activities. While I took care of the funeral itself, Janie took care of the reception that would be held in the parish hall. All of our relatives helped to decorate the hall with pictures of Mom and Dad. My brother put together a slide show of our family that ran all throughout the reception. My sister put together the music for the Mass. She even sang my dad's favorite hymn, the *Ave Maria.* I still don't know how she got through it without breaking down.

The hardest part of the day for me was having to give a eulogy for both of my parents, making sure that I treated them equally. When my brother and sister got into town, the three of us got together to share stories. I wanted to make sure that each of us was represented in the eulogy. As we shared stories, it became clear that we had drifted apart more than we knew. Since both of them lived outside of the area for the past ten years or so and seldom made visits to see Mom and Dad, they weren't aware of a lot of the things that they should have known as family members. This made me angry.

Both of them were obviously upset that Mom and Dad were gone, but I felt that it was more for show than real emotion. They had been separated too long. The day after the funeral we got together to go over Mom and Dad's will and gather what mementoes from the house we each wanted.

Lulu was staying at the house and boxed up the things that she wanted, which wasn't very much. Jake and his family were staying with us so Jake and I got to the house together. While I talked to LuLu, Jake made his way around the house selecting the things that he wanted. Once again, it was just one box of odds and ends. When I walked the house, there were so many memorable things left that it made me wonder what my brother and sister were thinking.

"LuLu, I thought that you liked Mom's cup and saucer collection? Don't you want it? What about her stuffed animal collection? You loved those animals as much as she did," I said excitedly.

"You know, Tom, I'm just not into collections at all. I have no place to put these things except to keep them in a box. You take them if you want them." She seemed sad.

"What about you, Jake? You always liked the ceramics that Dad painted. Don't you want any of them?" By this time, I was getting a little angry. How could they both be so callous as to not want to protect and honor our parents by taking the things that they used to like.

"Tom, that was a long time ago. Really, I don't want anything more than what I have in this box. Can we go now?" Both LuLu and Jake made their way to the door.

"Wait a minute, we haven't gone over the will yet. Don't you want to know what's in it?"

Jake answered angrily, "You know what's in it. You've been with Mom and Dad all this time and I'm sure that you'll be getting the lion's share of what there is to be had. Do you sign on their bank accounts?"

"Well, yes, but that was only for their protection since they were getting on in years. What do you really want to ask, Jake? Spit it out." Now I was just as angry as he was.

LuLu chimed in. "Do we really have to spell it out for you? Mom and Dad are gone and we're sure that you'll be throwing us a few crumbs just to keep us quiet while you take the largest piece of the pie for yourself. Isn't that so?"

I was appalled. How could my brother and sister think that I would do anything like that? "You're both out of your minds. I don't have any more claim to what Mom and Dad left than you do. We are family. I'm sure that Mom and Dad would want us to split the proceeds of their estate equally. Why don't we open the will and let that answer your questions?" This seemed to have calmed them down.

I opened the envelope containing the will that I had gotten from Mom and Dad's attorney the day before the funeral. There were strict instructions that the envelope not be opened until the day after the funeral with all three children present.

As all wills do, this one began with several paragraphs of legal speak that I just passed over. "Okay, here it is. 'We, Jack and Kate Simmons, being of sound mind do hereby bequeath the following to our son Tom to split as he sees fit amongst his brother, sister, and our grandchildren.'" My jaw dropped and I couldn't continue. There was no specific mention of anyone else in the will. It was all mine to do with as I pleased.

"Go on," LuLu spouted.

"Finish reading it," Jake added.

"I-I can't. It's unbelievable." I stood there looking at my brother and sister with the will held loosely at my side.

Jake took it from me and continued reading it. "'As Tom has cared for us during a good portion of our senior lives, and we have firm belief in his wisdom, he has the right to any and all funds accumulated in this estate. As for LuLu and Jake, we, as your parents, provided you with a home, a college education, and supported you through your many loves. We love you, but in your adult lives, you never returned our love. We have only seen our grandchildren twice since their birth and both times were when we made a trip to your homes.

"'Tom has cared for us and made sure that we wanted for nothing. For these reasons, it is only fitting that Tom disperse the proceeds of our estate as he sees fit.'"

"I don't believe this!" screamed LuLu. "What did they want from us? We have families that couldn't be pulled out of school whenever they wanted us to visit. Sure, we could have gone during the summer, but there was always someplace to go that had already been planned. This is totally unfair." She began to cry.

"Well, I pretty much knew it was going to go this way, but I never expected Mom and Dad to be so vindictive against us," Jake said shaking his head.

"Look, you guys, I know how difficult it is to make a long trip with kids when they are as young as ours are, but I'm pretty sure you could have made some sort of effort."

"Easy for you to say. You lived here with them. How many times have you been to our homes during the last ten years – three, four?"

"It doesn't matter how many times I came to see you. The point is that Mom and Dad felt slighted by both of you. Don't you think that they wanted to have a relationship with your kids other than greeting cards and presents on Christmas and birthdays? I'm pretty sure they would have loved that."

"I would have loved that, too, but it just didn't happen. What's the difference now? You have it all and that's the end of it." LuLu was dejected and turned to go.

"Wait, sis. Tom, what are your plans? You can't mean to keep it all for yourself, do you?" Jake walked toward me with an inquisitive look in his eyes. LuLu stopped, turned around, and looked at me with her piercing blue eyes.

"Of course not, but I feel as though I have to weigh what Mom and Dad's wishes were if I am to live up to their expectations."

"Well, I think that we both know what that means. You do what you have to and LuLu and I will do what we have to."

"What does that mean?" I asked not knowing what Jake was talking about.

"You're not the only one who can hire a lawyer to protect his interests." Jake and LuLu picked up their boxes and stormed out of the house.

I was astonished at their behavior. I tried putting myself in their shoes and just couldn't see myself acting that way. Maybe it was the guilt of being confronted by the truth. I didn't know. All I did know was that I didn't want our relationship to be damaged by greed.

They left that afternoon not saying goodbye, nor thank you, nor even staying for the family get together that we had planned for the next day. It was difficult explaining to aunts, uncles, and others who came from across the country why my brother and sister had to leave so soon.

By mid-November, I more firmly understood what the entirety of the estate was; it became clear to me what I needed to do, but before I did it, I wanted to ask Janie for her opinion.

The kids had just gone to bed and the house was quiet. Janie and I sat at the kitchen table with a cup of coffee munching on some cookies that she had baked with Nancy earlier in the day while Norman was at his piano lesson.

"Janie, I need to run something by you regarding my parents' estate. Do you mind listening to my proposal and giving me your honest opinion?" Being honest was never an issue with Janie.

"I can do that, Tom, but you know that you have the final decision in this. Your parents gave you that responsibility. I'm sure that whatever you came up with will be right for all of you. I trust you. Go ahead."

"Okay, so here it is. The estate comes up to approximately $325,000 if we get what the house is worth when we sell it. I want to give my brother and sister each $100,000 and we get $125,000."

"What about the grandchildren and why do we get the $25,000 extra?"

"Well, I was thinking that each family could distribute a portion of their share to their children as they see fit just as I have had to do. Maybe that will help them see the position that Mom and Dad put me in. The $25,000 helps us recover some of the money we spent since their death and a small stipend for me as executor. What do you think about that?"

Janie was not a 'yes' person. I asked for her opinion because I needed to get this right.

"Darling, you are such a good man. I actually think that you're being too generous to them. You and I spent a lot of time with your parents during the last few years of their life. That's time that we could have spent doing other things. Don't you think that we deserve some compensation for that?" I was totally shocked at Janie's opinion.

"Actually, sweety, I don't. I thought that what we did for them was out of love and not for some potential gain later on. I'm a little surprised that you think that way."

Janie put her hands across the table and took mine in hers. "You know that whatever you decide I'll support. Just don't sell yourself short. I know that you want to mend fences with Jake and LuLu, but it seems to me that if you want them to be an equal partner in this, they should at least apologize for their attitude before they left. They haven't even called to see how we are doing or even what you have decided. This has all been on your shoulders. I'm just saying that maybe they really don't deserve a full share. That's all."

I had to admit that she made sense, but to do anything else would mean straining our relationships even more than they already were.

"Okay, I'll pray on the matter." That was Dad's response whenever he had a tough decision to make. It seemed to help him and I was hoping that it would help me, too.

I prayed that night for guidance and asked myself 'what would Dad do?' I fell asleep without an answer. The next morning was Saturday and it dawned bright and clear. I usually got up around 9:00 on my days off, but not this Saturday. I woke up at 5:30 and could not go back to sleep so I got up and made my way into the computer room. I checked my email and Facebook account before I decided to email my brother and sister with an invitation.

LuLu and Jake,

I haven't heard from you since you left. I was wondering how you were feeling now that there has been some time to cool down. Did you really hire a lawyer? If you did, I haven't gotten any paperwork. I sincerely hope that you didn't. I'm sure that we can work this all out together as family.

Do you remember the Christmas Eve parties that Mom and Dad used to throw? I've been thinking about them lately and would like to get back to that tradition. I know that I can invite our friends from around here for a party, but I'd seriously like to have a Christmas Eve party with all of us to remember our own Christmases with Mom and Dad. I know that it will be fun for the kids. It will be the first time that they will all be together since the funeral. Wouldn't that be a nice way to remember Mom and Dad this Christmas? Please let me know if you will consider this. Let me know if you will be coming so that I can get Mom and Dad's house ready for you both to stay there. There's plenty of room now that I have it all cleaned out.

I miss you guys. We shouldn't be angry with each other. I love you both.

I didn't know if I would get any response from them, but within two days, I heard from both of them pretty much saying that they would consider it, but not to count on them being there. The messages were short and didn't give me hope that either of them would come.

By mid-December, I had given up on the idea of throwing a Christmas Eve party. I hadn't heard from either of them after that first message and I didn't want them to think that I was begging them to come. This would probably be the last time that we would be able to use Mom and Dad's house. I had it up for sale and there were some interested buyers. In any case, the house would be sold in the new year.

"Tom, have you heard from your brother or sister about your idea for a Christmas Eve party? You know it's only two days away and, if we're going to have a party, I have to get prepared. Don't you want to call them and see if you can get a firm answer? It's about time you talked to them anyway, don't you think?"

Janie was right. Email is not the same as a personal invitation. "I'll call in the morning. It's too late now."

I called each of them around 9:00, but no one was home so I left a brief message in voicemail asking if they were coming for Christmas Eve. I was pretty sure that they weren't coming so I told Janie not to worry about the party.

"If they were coming, we would have heard from them. It seemed like a good idea, but maybe just like they did to Mom and Dad, it's too much hassle to come and visit," I said sarcastically.

"Don't take that attitude. I thought that you got over last summer with them. Just forget it and call the kids for breakfast."

I awoke the morning of Christmas Eve to Christmas music playing with the kids and Janie singing along. I thought I'd have some fun so I yelled down the stairs, "Hey! Pipe down. Can't a guy get some sleep around here?" It was 8:30 and time to get up anyway. The next thing I heard were footsteps running up the stairs.

"Get up, Dad," Nancy squealed.

"C'mon, Pop. Don't sleep the day away. We want to go to I-Hop for blueberry peppermint pancakes."

Both kids jumped on the bed and proceeded to roll me off. We all laughed and I told them I'd be down in a minute and we'd go get those pancakes.

Janie came upstairs, wrapped her arms around my neck, and planted a long kiss on my lips. When she broke off the kiss, she said, "I love you, Mr. Simmons," and kissed me again.

"What was that for?" I asked.

"Oh, just because I wanted to. I really liked your idea of a Christmas Eve party so I thought that we'd go ahead and have one just for us. I already told the kids about Grandma and Grandpa's tradition and they're eager to keep it going even if it's just us."

I wasn't sure why Janie made up her mind to have a party on Christmas Eve Day, but it sounded as if the decision was made for me. "Okay, what do you want me to do?"

"Nothing. The kids and I will put it all together. Let's go get those pancakes."

I wasn't sure about blueberry and peppermint, but I have to admit that they were the best pancakes I'd ever had. After breakfast, I was sent on an errand to pick up some last-minute things for the party and Christmas dinner the next day.

Later in the afternoon, I had an idea that would make the party close to Mom and Dad's. "Honey, what do you say about going to Midnight Mass tonight? We used to do it with my parents. The kids are old enough. They should be able to stay awake. It's not like they have to go to bed early so that Santa can come. What do you say?" I didn't expect her to agree, but was pleasantly surprised when she did.

After dinner and the evening news, I put on my favorite Christmas movie, *It's a Wonderful Life*. The kids had never seen it. I wasn't sure if they would get it, but I told them what to look for and we discussed the characters as the movie played on. It was fun. They especially liked to 'boo' old man Potter just as they might have done in an early melodrama.

The movie had just finished and it was 8:00. Janie uncovered some cookies that she had baked earlier in the day and Norman got some mugs for cocoa, coffee, or eggnog. I had the eggnog. The kids had cocoa and Janie had a coffee. We four just sat on the couch and looked at the tree all decorated with ornaments from our past while listening to Christmas carols.

"We should have done this sooner," I said.

"This is a lot of fun. I wish the rest of the family could be here. Think how much fun it would be with all your cousins playing games and us adults yacking. Oh well, maybe next year," Janie responded.

Just then the doorbell rang. "I'll get it!" Nancy screamed.

"I wonder who that could be?" I asked.

"It may just be the neighbor bringing over some of her fruit cake. We've gotten one from her for the last three years, but we didn't get one yet this year."

"Fruitcake? I hate fruitcake," Norman said.

"Mom, Dad, look who's here!" squealed Nancy.

I couldn't believe my eyes. In walked Jake and his family. I just stood there with my mouth opened.

"Well, you said there was a party going on so we decided to surprise you, brother." Jake came right to me and gave me a big hug. He whispered in my ear, "You know I love you, Tom. I'm sorry for last summer. I trust that you'll do the right thing for all of us." He hugged me more firmly and I did as well.

Tears welled up in my eyes as my heart veritably leapt in my chest. My brother was here and it was just like old times. We got everybody's coats off, the kids went up to their bedroom to play games, and we all sat around the table talking about what had transpired since July. Just as I was about to tell Jake what I had decided regarding the estate, the doorbell rang again.

Janie went to answer it. I expected that it was the neighbor again with the elusive fruitcake.

"Hey, look who's here!" shouted Janie. In walked LuLu and her family. The kids didn't even wait to be told. As soon as they gave hugs, they were off to join their cousins.

"Hey, big brother. I like the way you decorated the outside of the house." Looking at the fireplace she said, "Where's the fire?" We all laughed. That was a reference to one Christmas Eve when I thought I was a 'lady's man' and smoked out the house during Midnight Mass.

That story was one worth retelling, so I did.

My parents and all our friends who were over for the annual Simmons Christmas Eve party went to Midnight Mass and a friend of mine who had a broken ankle stayed behind so I stayed to keep him company.

"Well, Mike, what do you say I make us a fire?"

"Sounds good. Need any help?"

"Nah, stay off your foot. I'll just go get some wood on the back porch."

When I got back, I was surprised to find two girls from the party entertaining Mike.

"Hey, girls, what's up? No more room in the church?" We had just met the two sisters at the party. They were relatives of one of my parents' friends visiting from Canada.

The older one, Marie, answered in her French-Canadian accent, "Plenty of room. We just didn't want you two to be lonely while everyone was gone." She smirked and her younger sister, Lanette, giggled. They were only a year apart and did everything together.

I put the wood down and we talked a little before Marie asked if there was anything to drink. She was about three years older than me and for the life of me I thought that she wanted a Coke or something.

When I offered it to her, she said, "That will be good if you have some rum to put in it."

Now I was beginning to get the idea. "I'm sure we have some around here somewhere." My parents weren't drinkers so I wasn't sure we had any, but I guess they bought some for the party because there it was right on the kitchen sink.

I brought her the bottle and started pouring the rum into a glass filled with ice when she put her hand on mine and simply said, "Enough." You can guess where my thoughts ran as I filled the rest of the glass with Coke.

Lanette and Mike had been chatting and she was in the process of writing a message on his cast when Mike said, "Hey, Tom, what about that fire?"

"Yea, right." I picked up the wood, made a chimney wood stack as I learned in Boy Scouts, got some newspaper, crumpled it up and put it in the middle of the chimney. I had to look in four drawers in the kitchen before I found the matches.

I lit the paper and it did what it was supposed to do, light the wood on fire. While the fire was starting, Mike and I sat next to the sisters and were just about to make our move when smoke started billowing out of the fireplace. The house filled with smoke in no time. We all raced around the house opening every window and door to let the smoke get out before my parents and everybody got home.

Marie said, "What happened? Haven't you ever made a fire before?" The truth was that I had never made a fire in our fireplace. How was I to know that the flu needed to be opened to let the smoke rise up the chimney? We laughed and chatted as the fire died out and the smoke poured out of the house.

"Do you remember that?" I asked Jake and LuLu.

"Yea, but I don't remember the story happening quite that way. What I remember is you telling us that…"

Jake went on to tell the story with minor variations and we all laughed trying to determine what the real story was.

"You guys are both wrong. This is how it happened." And LuLu gave her rendition. More laughter.

While we all remembered that story, it was the first time that our spouses ever heard it. Talk about being confused. I think that by the end of LuLu's version, they were just happy that it was over and that I didn't burn the house down.

The night went on and around 11:00 we gathered the kids up and all went to Midnight Mass. I can't speak for anyone else, but my heart swelled with love for my family as we all shared one pew, and received the Lord in the Eucharist.

When we got back to the house, we opened gifts, had one more cup of cocoa, and then sent the kids off to bed. They had brought their sleeping bags so it was going to be an in-house campout. They loved it.

Janie finished cleaning the kitchen and went up to bed, leaving the three of us to share our memories of Christmases past with Mom and Dad.

Jake, LuLu, and I stayed up and chatted for another hour or so. It was great. Finally, I said, "By the sounds of it, we are all good. Am I right?"

LuLu answered first. "Tom, we are family and I know that whatever you decide will be fine. I don't know what came over me at the house last July. I miss Mom and Dad and I'm sad that they felt the way they did about us. I wish I could do it all over again, but I can't. I'll just accept your judgment."

"I feel the same way. We have too much history to throw our relationship away because of money. I love you, brother." With that, we all gathered together and had a group hug.

Finally, I broke away from the hug and said, "Well, I'm glad that you feel that way because my decision is that you're each getting nothing."

They both just stood there ready to argue with me when I couldn't stand it any longer. "No, no I'm just kidding." I explained the split with them on the approximate value and they were both very happy.

I think that we got stronger as a family for having gone through the trial of Mom and Dad's death and distribution of the estate. I know that I am happier now than I have been in a long time. In fact, we decided to rotate Christmas Eve parties and not make any excuses for not being there.

Well, now you know my story.

"Kids, are you ready? Time to leave for Uncle Jake's," I yelled up the stairs.

"Coming, Dad. Where's Mom?"

"Already in the car. Let's go."

By the way, the house sold for a lot more than we figured so I split the new figure in thirds and didn't take anything extra for myself.

What else can I say, but have a Merry Christmas and a Happy New Year!

Day Four
Mama's Night Out

It was just one of those nights that I just couldn't decide whether to go home or sleep at the office. It's not that my case load was that big, but just that it was Christmas Eve and I had no one at home waiting for me – no lights, no presents under the tree, not even a tree. I'm not a Scrooge or anything like that, but I just couldn't get into the spirit of Christmas this year.

I'm a private investigator and I had been working a case that just made me sick. I was just about done with the final report when I realized that it was Christmas Eve. The antique grandfather clock in the corner was chiming seven. This clock was all that I had left of my childhood – no brothers or sisters, parents gone, no property. It made me flash back to Christmases past. Some good, some not so good. Anyway, the rest of the offices in the building had been closed for hours. Everyone had gone home for the holiday, but here I stayed. Maggie, my receptionist, left around noon with my good wishes.

Why go home? What was the point? I would only be reminded of the Christmases past when I did have the spirit. I opened the bottom drawer of my desk and pulled out a bottle of Christmas cheer. I turned on the radio and found some Christmas music. The lights were intentionally dim, as I tend to think better that way.

I was on my third or fourth glass of 'cheer' and Bing Crosby was reminding me of the White Christmas I've never had when the office door opened.

"Sorry, it's Christmas Eve. I'm not open. Just finishing up some paperwork," I yelled.

There wasn't a sound from the locked outer office. I was sure that I heard someone come in. "Is there anyone there?" I shouted. No answer.

I decided I'd better check it out. As soon as I tried to get out of the chair, I knew that I was a little drunk. I hadn't eaten lunch or dinner and now I was paying for it. I felt dizzy and tripped over my own feet as I tried to get to the outer office. As I grabbed for the corner of the desk to steady myself, my hand slipped off of it and I went sprawling to the floor.

I was still on the floor when I came to. I thought it odd that the clock was chiming seven again. The office was dark and cold and I had a major headache.

I pulled myself to my knees and noticed that the neon sign from the drug store across the street wasn't blinking its 'Open 24 Hours' message. The room also smelled musty like it hadn't been cleaned in a long time.

As I made my way to the light switch, I bumped into a chair that shouldn't have been in the way. I found the wall and, ultimately, the switch. In the dark, I could tell that the switch was just like the ones in my grandparents' apartment when I was just a kid. I pressed it on and was not prepared for what I saw. This was my office, but it wasn't. What was going on here?

The soft ceiling light had been changed to a bare 100-watt bulb. The light hurt my eyes so I covered them with my arm until I got used to the brightness. After a minute or so, I was able to see that my office had been transformed into a 1940s Sam Spade replica. I rubbed my eyes hoping to see my real office when I opened them again. No luck.

I went to the window that had now been covered with a plain green window shade instead of the drapes that were there before I fell. I opened the shade and froze at the sight. Montgomery Street, San Francisco, had been transformed into a 1940s scene – complete with cars and extras. As if that wasn't enough of a shock, my reflection in the window told me that I wasn't really me. I mean, it was the same face, but the clothes were all wrong.

I made my way back to the chair behind my old oak desk that fit the 1940s. The chair had changed from a big heavy comfortably padded chair to a wooden chair on wheels that matched the desk. The rug had also disappeared to reveal a hardwood floor. What was going on? I had no clue. It was like I had been transported back in time. Then I heard the door to the outer office open.

"Who's there? What are you pulling here?" I demanded.

The sound of high heels was unmistakable. The scent of lavender was overwhelming and the beauty of the woman standing in front of me was captivating from her veiled pillbox hat down to her flame red dress, nails and lips, seamed stockings, and spiked red heels that matched her dress. This seemed like a woman worth knowing.

She turned the veil up on her head to reveal a face worthy of the outfit she wore. "Mr. Donavan, I hope I'm not too late. I know that it's Christmas Eve, but I have to see you. It's a matter of life and death."

It looked like she had been crying. I guess the investigator in me took over. I had to know more about this bewitching woman.

"Don't worry about it being Christmas Eve. I can tell that you are in some distress. Why don't you sit down and tell me what the problem is. Can I get you some coffee or something stronger?" I sincerely hoped that she would say no to the coffee. I would have to make some.

"No, that's okay. I just can't believe my luck in finding you here tonight. I didn't know where else to go. I've been walking the streets for the last five hours. I must have passed your building at least a dozen times before I got up enough courage to come up. I almost wished that you weren't going to be here so I could just forget the whole deal, but I didn't give up and here I am and there you are."

Now that was a mouthful and I wasn't sure that I understood what she meant by all of it, but I was going to find out. "Let's take it slow. First, just call me Mike. I don't stand on formalities. And, who might you be?"

She stared at me for a moment before speaking. "I'm sorry. I thought you knew. I thought that's why you stayed here tonight." Now I was really confused. I had to be smart if I wanted to continue this conversation.

"Well, you can't ever be too careful. Have you ever met me before? How do you know I'm Mike Donavan?" It was a gamble, but it seemed to be a fair one.

"No, I've never met you, but…" She clammed up and looked around the office as though she expected someone else to be there. After satisfying herself that we were alone, she caught my gaze and never let me go. As our eyes danced with each other, she slipped her hand into the purse she carried. I wasn't sure what she was getting, but I was willing to let her play the hand.

Out came the reason that she came to my office that Christmas Eve. At first, I thought it was a toy. It blinked green and red as it sparkled and made a whirring sound.

Even without knowing her name, I had to know what she had taken out of her purse. "What is that? It's not a gun, is it?"

The mystery woman looked at me with some surprise. "This is what we want you to protect until ten tonight. It would be disastrous if this ever got into the wrong hands."

Logic kicked in and I had to ask, "If you've been carrying this around all afternoon, why can't you just keep it? What's the life and death matter you spoke of? What is that thing and who are you anyway?"

I moved toward her, she dropped the whirly-gig thing on the chair and ran out. I chased after her, but could not catch her. In fact, I couldn't even hear her heels down the darkened hallway. She seemed to be gone in an instant.

I thought that I was confused before she walked into my office, but now I had no idea what was going on. One more shot of booze helped calm me down and I decided that I had to attack one mystery at a time.

I always checked the latest news on the Internet in the morning. I figured I'd just check the web and see if there were any film companies working in San Francisco on

Christmas Eve. I turned from the door and noticed that my computer was missing. On the credenza to the rear of my desk where the computer should have been was now a newspaper. I made my way over to the paper not really wanting to look at it, but, after all that had just happened, pretty sure what I would find.

I was right. It was 24 December 1947. My legs grew weak and I sat back in my chair. Was this really happening to me or was it a dream borne from the concussion I must have gotten when I fell to the floor? It sure seemed real. I shook my head. Nothing changed. The paper was still there. The office was still decorated in 1940s furniture and I was still wearing that baggy gray suit with wide lapels.

As if I knew what I would find, I searched the jacket pocket for my cell phone. Nope, but there on the desk was an ancient black rotary phone. I picked up the receiver to listen for dial tone. It was there so I tried calling Maggie, my receptionist. No luck. I hung up and sat on the desk trying to figure out what that whirly-gig thing was.

I didn't know what was going on, but I did know that I couldn't do anything about it no matter what it was. It became apparent to me that I couldn't just sit in the office and wait for something to happen. I had been dealt a hand to play by the mysterious lady in red and I was going to see it through. I picked up the whirly-gig and inspected it. I had never seen anything like it in my life.

I tucked it away in my overcoat pocket and made my way to the lobby. I had to take the stairs down four flights because the elevator operator had gone for Christmas and the gate was drawn and locked.

I left the building and thought I'd hole up at Millie's Coffee Shop to think this thing out. She served the best zucchini bread in town so it was a no-brainer. Besides, I was hungry anyway. I wasn't sure what I would find. I knew that Millie's had been there a long time, but I wasn't sure if it had been there in 1947. I was in luck.

Not only was Millie's still there, but it was even open at 8:45 on Christmas Eve. I pushed the door open and the bell at the top of the door tinkled to let the waitress know that someone had just entered. She wasn't familiar, but I could tell she really didn't want to be there.

She broke her scowl from the end of the horseshoe counter and said, "Just coffee or are ya gonna make me wake up the cook?"

I could tell that this was not going to go well. "Just coffee and a piece of your zucchini bread if you have any."

"How do you know about my zucchini bread? I only make that for friends. We don't serve it here at the diner." She moved closer and I could see that her nametag said "Millie." The restaurant was now known as 'Stan's Diner'. Just another fact to turn my world upside down.

Not wanting to get in a row, I just went with the flow. "I'm sorry. I thought that you served it here. Someone in the elevator was talking about the best zucchini bread in town and mentioned your name. No problem. I'll have whatever is easy for you."

"It'll be just a minute. I have to make a fresh pot of coffee." She walked into the kitchen and I was left alone at the counter with my thoughts.

As I was pondering my next move, several other people walked into the diner. I turned my head and was surprised to see that they were all little people about four feet tall or so. There must have been six or seven of 'em and they were all wearing trench coats. They sat in the two booths behind me.

Millie came out of the kitchen with a steaming cup of coffee and a slice of zucchini bread. "I just happened to have some in the back that I baked special for Stan. He's asleep. He'll never miss it if you know what I mean." Millie winked and I knew that Stan must have been sleeping it off in the back.

"I'll be right with you, boys," Millie called over the counter.

Then, in the squeakiest voice I'd ever heard, the tall one (about 4'2") said, "It's okay, lady. We just want some information. Have you seen a classy lassy parading 'round the streets in a bright red dress? She was supposed to meet us, but we ain't seen her and it's important we meet up with her before ten tonight."

I was interested as to what Millie's answer would be. She said, "She was in here. She also mentioned something about ten tonight. She asked if I knew some gumshoe named Donavan. I never heard of the guy, but I told her to check out the buildings across the way. Seems I heard that those types have offices over there."

The little guys started talking amongst themselves in a language I had never heard before. The tall one turned to Millie, "If she comes back, would you tell her that all is forgiven and we want her to come back? Can you do that?"

"I guess I can. Whom should I say asked for her and what's her name?"

More foreign talk then the one that was closest to the aisle slid out of his seat and hiked himself up on the counter stool right in front of Millie. He leaned in and, almost in a whisper said, "Let's just say that this is a case of national security and keep it at that, can we?"

"Sure, mister. How do I get in touch with you?" Millie was now visibly shaken.

"We're gonna keep searching for her, but we'll check in every once in a while. If she shows up, try and serve her some of this hot chocolate. It's her favorite." The little guy pulled out a thermos and laid it on the counter.

As I was watching the encounter, a tap came on my opposite elbow. "What's your interest in this, buddy?" squeaked a different little person trying to be intimidating.

"No interest – just curious. Maybe I've seen this mystery woman." In unison, all of their seven heads snapped in my direction.

"Okay, mister. What do you think you know? And you better not be playing with us 'coz we don't have time to be chasing after ghosts."

I wasn't sure what I was doing, but it seemed that I'd get closer to an answer on my mystery lady if I engaged the little buggers rather than sneak out and away from them.

"Well, first let me ask you a few questions. Seems to me that you have enough guys here to search at least seven blocks at the same time, but here you sit all seven of you in the same diner. Are you that convinced that she's around here somewhere?"

The tall one whirled his seat around, leaned in, and said, "We don't have to tell you anything. Do you have any information for us or not? If not, quit wasting our time."

I stared him straight in the eyes waiting to see who'd blink first. He never blinked so I gave in to move the conversation along. "I saw this gal in red heading for the trolley about a half hour ago. It could be her. She had something blinking in her hand. That's how I remember her. What was that thing and who is she?"

More foreign conversation and all the guys got out of the booths and surrounded me. "I think you'd better come with us," said the leader. "It's obvious to me that you know more than you're letting on."

I had overplayed my hand and was now in deep trouble. If they decided to search me, I'd have to fight them off. I knew I could take two or three of them, maybe even four or five, but I was pretty sure that I couldn't handle all seven of them. I had to think quickly or be prepared for the consequences.

"Why would I want to go with you? I don't even know who you are. Do you have a badge or something? As far as I know, you're some kind of foreign agents. I don't understand that lingo you keep yakkin'. Millie, call the cops." This seemed to have done the trick. I had called their bluff.

They all started chattering at once. While I couldn't make it all out, one of them plainly said, "We don't need no stinkin' badges."

Then the youngest little person piped up, "Gee, mister, we're not bad guys. We just want to get Mama back to Nick by ten."

"That'll be enough out of you," spat the leader. "Go ahead, call the cops. In the meantime, I'll take what you have in your pocket."

For some reason, the whirly-gig had started spinning and flashing. He must have seen it. We must have stared at each other for a good fifteen seconds when the leader shouted, "Get him, boys!"

The battle was fierce. I no sooner kicked one of them aside and another would take his place. Just as I had guessed, I couldn't fight off seven of those little guys. There I was, a grown man lying on the diner floor with little guys sitting on my arms and legs and one fishing through my pockets.

Just as they were about to hit pay dirt, a beat cop came charging into the place. "Alright, you guys! Break it up! What's this all about then?" Mike Flannigan was new to the beat and very Irish. He had his orders to keep the peace and that's just what he was going to do.

I know they felt the device in my pocket, but were afraid to take it out in front of Officer Flannigan. I decided to play a hunch. "Officer, it's okay. We were just arguing about the merits of Santa Claus and these lads took exception to my notion that there is no Santa Claus."

"Is that right, boys?" Officer Flannigan looked a little disbelieving.

"That's right."

"Yeah!"

"Sure!"

"That's it!" they all blurted out at the same time. "Just a big misunderstanding."

They let me up and brushed the dust off of my suit.

Flannigan looked over at Millie who just shrugged her shoulders. "Well, I don't know which of you has been drinkin' the most, but I'm giving you only this one warning.

You're lucky that none of this furniture got broken or I'd be runnin' the lot of you in for drunk and disorderly. You boys take your fun to someone else's block." On his way out the door, he turned around, looked at the scene one more time, and simply said, "Merry Christmas."

He exited the diner, stopped in front of the plate glass window, and peered in to make sure that we wouldn't start up scuffling again.

The leader who had found the device in my pocket turned to me, "Okay, mister. You seem to think you have this thing figured out. So, why don't you just give us the 'Matter-Smatter' and we'll be on our way with you none the wiser. Believe me, it's better for you if you don't know what's going on."

"Why don't you let me be the judge of that? Now, who are Mama and Nick? And don't tell me a mob guy and his mother. Tell me the truth. By the way, how long did you think that those trench coats would hide your elf costumes?" It wasn't just the costumes that gave them away. It was mostly their pointy ears.

It was when we were fighting that I noticed flashes of red and green and things started falling into place – even though it was a place I didn't want to go.

"Millie, I think you can dump that hot chocolate these boys gave you. Millie? Millie!" There was no answer so I went back into the kitchen and there was Millie sound asleep with a half cup of hot chocolate in front of her. Just as I had suspected – the cocoa was doped.

I left the kitchen, took out the "Matter-Smatter," and placed it on the counter. "Now, do you want to tell me what this is and what it has to do with the lady in red or do I call

Officer Flannigan back in here? I'm sure that he's probably not too far down the block."

The leader took a position in front of his men. "Okay, you win. Time's getting short and it looks like whether I like it or not, we need you to help us save Christmas."

Saving Christmas was not exactly what I expected to hear. "What exactly are you talking about? Christmas is less than three hours away. Packages have been bought, trees have been decorated, and lights have been blinking for weeks. What do you mean that you need me to help save Christmas? Christmas is tomorrow."

The leader took the 'Matter-Smatter' from the counter. "Here's how it works. First, you have to believe or it will never work. Then you have to set a specific time that you want to leave and return."

"Wait a minute! What are you talking about? Is this some sort of time machine?" I couldn't believe that I was even asking this question. I didn't believe in time travel or Santa Claus either.

"Sort of. It only works for those that truly believe."

"Believe in what? The sun, the moon, the earth is round?" I was getting sarcastic in my frustration to understand. "Help me out here. Give me a clue?"

The leader turned to the rest of the elves and muttered in gibberish to them. "Okay, here it is. Santa and Mrs. Claus had a spat and she took off with his 'Matter-Smatter', the very same 'Matter-Smatter' that Santa uses on Christmas Eve to deliver all his toys around the world. It works like a time machine except with the added bonus of being able to molecularly alter gifts by Santa's thought waves."

"What does all of that even mean? I don't get it. First of all, I'm not a believer so this will be hard for you to prove to me."

"We don't need to prove anything to you. I'm telling you what is happening and that you have the opportunity to help us save not only this Christmas, but all future Christmases. Mrs. Claus, your lady in red, took the 'Matter-Smatter' in a huff to teach Santa a lesson. She's really a wonderful woman, but she's gone off the deep end on this one."

For a non-believer, I sure had a lot of questions. "So, why did she leave Santa? Was he abusive? Is there another elf? How am I supposed to believe any of this and, if I do end up believing what you're telling me, what do you want me to do to help?"

"It's simple. I have the 'Matter-Smatter' and that's great, but Santa wants Mama back. His work at Christmas won't mean the same to him without Mama there to help by keeping his chocolate warm and him awake on the big night."

"So, now I'm confused again. Does Mrs. Claus go with Santa on his ride around the world?" I couldn't believe that I even asked that question. Even though I didn't believe, I had to hear the end of this story.

"I told you that Santa delivers gifts by transference of thought waves via the 'Matter-Smatter' to the homes he wants. He never leaves the North Pole workshops."

"So there is no sleigh and reindeer trotting the globe on Christmas Eve?"

All of the elves started chuckling, "Of course not. That whole concept was a slick Madison Avenue trick to get kids to ask their parents for toys at Christmas. Santa can't stand 'Rudolph the Red-Nosed Reindeer' and 'The Night Before Christmas.' Here's how it works. The 'Matter-Smatter' suspends time on one night a year; Christmas Eve. That's all the power it has. Once time is suspended, Santa reads his list and telepathically sends his gifts to each girl and boy who believes."

As funny as it may sound, it all made perfect sense, but why me? How did I get involved in this mess? "So how is it that Mama is such a 'Hot Mama' and how did she know to come looking for me and why did she only want me to hold this until ten tonight?"

"She said that? Only until ten?" The gibberish continued in the back row.

"Well, that's good news. If Mama only wanted you to hold this until 10:00, it proves that she was planning on getting back to Santa before the midnight deadline. If she was later than midnight, Santa would not be able to make his Christmas run. I told you she's a good old bird."

"So, if she was planning on going back at ten anyway, why get me involved? Is there something else you're not telling me?"

The leader put his hand on my wrist and pulled me down to whisper in my ear. All I could say in response was, "I see. I had no idea. It does make perfect sense."

At that moment, Mama walked into the diner. "Have you boys had your fun chasing after me all night? I told you that you'd never catch me. I was right. I was also right to pick this Mr. Donavan to be my accomplice. From the looks of you boys, he gave you all you could handle."

I sat flabbergasted on a stool at the counter. Mrs. Claus was still a knockout in her red dress. I couldn't believe what was about to happen. As the lead elf had whispered in my ear, Mrs. Claus would need to give me a kiss before she could return to the North Pole.

It appeared that this play happened every year. Each Christmas Eve, Santa picked one person who was missed on a Christmas past to let him or her know that he was sorry he missed him that Christmas Eve so many years ago. The hard part for Santa was getting the person to believe that he still remembered him so he got his elves and Mrs. Claus to help him.

She moved across the floor like a dream, stopped at my stool, put her hand on the back of my neck, and gave me the best kiss I ever had. It literally knocked me out.

When I awoke, I was back in my office sitting in the chair – the stuffed chair. The neon light blinked through the curtains. My email memo beeper was going off and I had the most terrible headache I'd ever had.

The clock chimed ten and I remembered – remembered it all. In 1947, I didn't get any toys because we were too poor and Santa didn't know where we lived. We moved a lot in those days. I was ten at the time and wasn't sure if I believed in Santa or not. Apparently, I was taken back to 1947 for a Christmas kiss so that Santa could let me know that, even though I may not believe in him, he still believed in me.

How corny could I get? What was I thinking? There was no 'Matter-Smatter' and Mrs. Claus didn't look like a supermodel. And, of course, Rudolph guided Santa's sleigh every Christmas to bring toys to good little girls and boys.

I had just about convinced myself that my memories were dreams from the concussion I must have gotten when I fell. I got out of the chair and looked in the mirror for the bump I expected to see on my head. I was surprised to not only find the bump, but ruby red lipstick smeared on my lips.

I gazed at myself in disbelief. My head hurt worse than ever. I was thinking too much. There had to be an explanation. I stared and stared at that lipstick. Someone must have tried to give me mouth-to-mouth resuscitation – that's it. That's where the lipstick came from.

I made my way back to the desk. I felt good about my answer until I opened my email. All it said was 'Merry Christmas,' which wasn't strange at all. It was the sender that made me wonder all over again exactly what had happened to me that night. The signature simply read, 'Mama.'

Day Five
The Best Gift of All

It would be our first Christmas alone together. No, not our first year together, but our fiftieth. We had always been around family at Christmas. For the first three years of our marriage, it was Maggie's and my parents and both of our brothers and sisters and their families. Then we were blessed with our own family.

Jamie, Joan, and John came along within the next three years – *Bing, Bang, Boom!* Christmases from that point on were a blur of gift buying, sledding, baking, tree decorating, Midnight Masses, Christmas mornings, and Christmas dinners with family invited over. Maggie's two sisters always helped by bringing over a dessert or a favorite casserole (usually green bean) to share. They helped set the tables (one main and the kids' table), put out the snacks, made sure that everyone had something to drink, and took care of everyone at the party. At times, it seemed as though we may have been at their own homes.

Maggie is a great cook and she always outdid herself at Christmas. We knew that our turkey and ham dinner would be fantastic, but she always added something special that none of us knew about. In fact, the only ones that knew what was going to be presented were her two sisters. The rest of us were kept in the dark.

My part in all this was to carve the turkey and the ham. Maggie and her sisters made sure that I didn't have any access to the specialty of the year. When dinner was ready, no one had to be asked twice to come to the dinner table. Kids came in from the playroom and outside. The adults came in from the living room, not much caring that the Cowboys were once again getting their spurs handed to them by the Packers.

Everyone had to sit down first before any of the food would be brought out. It was a tradition that Maggie started at either our third or fourth family Christmas dinner. One of the three sisters would pop out of the kitchen door and check to see that all was set for the grand entrance. Once all were seated, the presentation, for that's what it really was, began.

First, the rolls with honey butter specially whipped by Maggie's sister, Jeanette, were placed on the tables. Then two kinds of cranberry sauce were brought out. There was cranberry jelly from a can and real homemade cranberry sauce made by my sister, Jackie. It didn't take long for the rest of the usual dinner foods to make their way to the tables – salad, mashed potatoes dripping with butter, sweet potatoes snow topped with marshmallow, bread stuffing, turkey, ham, and various holiday vegetables and casseroles. As if this weren't enough for each of us to get our fill, there was always one last special dish and it changed every year.

On our tenth year of hosting Christmas dinner, it was a dish called "Christmas Franks and Beans." Go ahead, laugh. But I want to tell you that you haven't tasted anything like Maggie's Christmas Franks and Beans. Besides the obvious franks and beans, there was something special that was mixed into the beans that gave it a Christmas flavor. Some didn't even want to try it, but for those of us who knew that Maggie would never serve anything that wasn't great, we jumped at the new dish first right after saying Grace. What was that Christmas flavor? It was so familiar yet new to our palettes. Finally, Maggie's mom figured it out.

"Peppermint!" she shouted. "It's peppermint! How did you do that?" The rest of the family all chimed in with their agreement that it indeed was peppermint in the franks and beans.

Maggie shared her process. "I did a little experimenting during our Fourth of July barbecue and found that melting peppermint white chocolate and crushed peppermint sticks into the beans gave me the flavor I was looking for. As soon as I tasted it, I knew that when I threw in some franks, I would have my Christmas dish. Do you like it?"

She knew that they would be honest and they were.

Uncle Fred was always the most critical. He had to have a salad bowl when everyone else put their salad on the plate with the rest of the meal. He had to have the crust trimmed from his bread. He couldn't have any ice in his cold (or not so cold) drinks. He was just a finicky guy. So, when he clinked his glass of ice-less water to get attention, everyone was prepared for the worst.

In his crustiest voice he said, "I don't know what on earth made you think that you could put chocolate and peppermint into beans and franks and make something Christmasy out of it. No chef in his right mind would even think of that." I could see Maggie's head and shoulders droop as she prepared herself for the death blow that Uncle Fred was preparing to administer.

"Now, Fred," interrupted his wife, Blanche. "You know that Maggie has never failed to make something spectacular for our Christmas dinner. Why do you have to be that way?"

"Blanche, why don't you let me finish what I was trying to say? You always have to butt in when you don't even know what I'm going to say." He shook his head and continued. "As I was saying, no chef in his right mind would ever think of putting peppermint into franks and beans for part of a Christmas dinner. It's only our Maggie with her flair for the 'unusual' that can take something so common and make it so delicious. Mags, can you give that recipe to Blanche? That's good enough to eat all year 'round."

The family exploded into cheers and positive comments. They all wanted the recipe.

"I'll get it together and email it out to all of you. I'm glad you liked it, Uncle Fred. I was a bit worried there for a minute."

Fred just smiled and said, "You know I can't just up and say when something is good. I have to give you a little grief along the way. It wouldn't be me otherwise." The whole family laughed and dinner continued with comments of how good everything was.

Following dinner, the kids would retire to one of their bedrooms to play games, the wives and some of the girls would clean up the kitchen, and us guys would have an after-dinner drink, sit, and watch either a football or basketball game on the tube. It was the same every year and Christmas Day dinner grew to be close to thirty-five people with sons, daughters, new husbands and wives, and even a few neighbors thrown in.

Then about ten years ago, Maggie's mom died and my dad died. Both died right around Thanksgiving within two weeks of each other. Needless to say, it was a sad time for all and, even though we knew that it would be good for the whole family to be together again on Christmas Day, Maggie just couldn't pull herself together to agree to host it again. No amount of coaxing from her two sisters and me could change her mind so we decided to not have a big dinner, but just have an open house where people could just pop in for a little while and leave when they wanted. We put out a store-bought deli platter, snacks, and had drinks available. The only home-made item was a soup that Maggie made from scratch. It was a vegetable soup, but with big chunks of vegetables and special seasonings. A bowl of her soup was a meal in itself.

After Christmas, Maggie and I talked about the difference on Christmas Day without our parents around. Maggie agreed that it was a mistake to not have the dinner. Both her mom and my dad would have wanted the dinner to go on to bring the family together. We vowed to continue the tradition the next year. Unfortunately, sometimes when you break a tradition, new ones take its place. And that's exactly what happened the next year. New Christmas Day dinner traditions were started all across the family so that when we invited them back for Christmas dinner, there was only a fraction of the family that could come.

None of Maggie's sisters were coming. They now had their own kids helping to prepare Christmas dinner. The kids seemed glad to be staying at home. One thing that didn't change was the special Christmas dish that Maggie made each year. In fact, that tradition carried on to the rest of the family. Each Christmas dinner had the special flavor of the cook incorporated into the main meal or dessert. Each year thereafter, all of the special dishes would find themselves in an email to the rest of the family.

Year after year, part of the family dwindled away. Some of them moved away, others made other plans, and some scheduled Christmas vacations away from town. Last year was the worst. Only John and his wife came to dinner. Both of their kids were having Christmas dinner with their own spouses' families.

"Well, guess this is the last year we do Christmas dinner," Maggie mused to herself while swirling gravy through her mashed potatoes with a fork.

"What do you mean? We've always had Christmas dinner here. It won't be the same without it." John looked at his wife, Nancy.

"Mom, you know how much we love your dinner and especially your special dish. It's a tradition. You can't just not do it." Nancy was mouthing the words, but her heart wasn't in it. In fact, she and John had other plans also, but changed them when they found out that no one else would be coming to dinner.

"Anyway, what's the special dish this year?" Nancy asked.

"Since there was only going to be four of us, I made a special dessert. I hope you like it. I'll serve it after the dishes and while we're gaping at the tube." We finished our dinner in relative silence with the occasional, "Please pass the 'whatever.'" It got passed and the clinking of utensils on china continued.

When dinner was finished, both John and Nancy helped Maggie with the dishes. I poured myself a Chivas on the rocks and turned on the TV and there they were, just like so many Christmases past, the Lakers kicking the snot out of some other pathetic team. I think it was the Kings' turn this year.

"John," Maggie asked, "why do you think that no one wants to come for dinner anymore? Is it something we've done or not done? I understand that there is now a whole extended family that has grown out of our core family, but you and Nancy were the only ones that were even interested."

John felt ashamed. Should he tell his mother the truth or share a falsehood with her. She had raised him well so he knew that the truth was the only option. "Mom, the truth is that we've all moved on with our lives and have more than just our family to consider. We had fun and enjoyed ourselves all those years we had Christmas dinner over here, but those days are gone and in the past. Since I'm being honest with you, you should know that Nancy and I were invited over to Zack's house for dinner. We're going there when we leave here for a second dinner and to open presents with him and the rest of his family. It will be just like when we used to do that here, but now it's with our own families. It's almost like it used to be, but without you and Dad there."

Maggie understood what John was saying, but that didn't stop her heart from aching for the days when she and her cooking were all the talk of Christmas day.

"You're right, John. Some traditions don't last forever and some get changed as they grow. This is just the way it has to be from now on, I guess. Thanks for being honest with me. You and Nancy should head on over to Zack's now."

John interrupted, "No, Mom. We haven't had your special dessert yet. We can't leave without having some. We don't even know what it is."

Maggie got up from the kitchen table where they were both sitting. Nancy had joined me for the basketball game after she wiped the last pan.

"Here," Maggie went to the fridge and took out a Pyrex baking pan covered in tin foil with her special Christmas dessert in it. "Take this along with a quart of vanilla ice cream to go on top. It's called 'Christmas Pear Trifle.' I'll send out the recipe on the email like I always do. Take it and share it with your son and his family. Let me know how they liked it."

John took the dessert, reached into the freezer for the ice cream, kissed his mother on the cheek, and came out to say goodbye and tell Nancy that it was time to go. Nancy got up, asked what was in the bag, got her jacket, gloves, scarf, and hat, kissed us goodbye, and off they went.

"What happened?" I curiously asked. "Why did they leave without tasting your dessert?" I hadn't asked what was in the bag.

"It was time. That's all. They really needed to be with Zack and his family today. I gave them the Christmas Pear Trifle that I made this year." She choked off a little sadness as she explained.

"Come here. Let me hold you. It'll be alright." She came to me, cuddled into my shoulder and began to sob. "We had a good run. I guess it's time to find some new traditions to start. Maybe we'll go on vacation next year at Christmas. It seems that there's nothing to keep us here."

Maggie wiped a tear from her eye, "I don't know, Mike. It's too soon to think about that. Maybe it will be different next year." She began sobbing again.

"Maybe," was all I could think of to say.

So here we were one year later and it's the week after Thanksgiving. Each of the kids invited us over for Thanksgiving, but at the risk of alienating one or the other of them, we stayed home and Maggie cooked us a turkey breast with all the fixins. We watched all the parades and most of the football games.

"So, are we going on vacation this Christmas like we talked about last year?" It was the first time that I had brought it up since last Christmas.

"I don't know, Mike. The kids may want to come over for dinner and I'd hate to disappoint them."

"Have you asked them to come over yet? Who's coming?" I really wanted to know.

"Well, no one has said they would come, but that doesn't mean that they won't."

"Have any of them asked us over for Christmas dinner?" That was the question that I really wanted answered.

"No, I think that they think I'll be cooking and that others will be coming over. So, no, we haven't gotten an invitation yet."

I really didn't want her to be disappointed again as she was last year so I pressed on with the vacation plans. "You know, it would be great to get out of the snow one Christmas and see what the other side of the country does on Christmas without any snow. What do you say?"

I was surprised. It didn't take Maggie long at all to simply say, "Where are we going?"

I hadn't expected it to be this easy so I blurted out the first thing that came into my head, "We're going to Disneyland!"

She giggled and said, "Oh, you are still the big kid I married. I love you. That's a great idea. I can't wait." Then she hugged and kissed me just as though we were two crazy kids who had just decided to go on a date to the "Happiest Place on Earth." All that was left was to make the reservations and tell the kids.

Making the reservations was no big deal, but telling the kids was more difficult than we thought. We couldn't decide if Maggie or I would tell them. Finally, two weeks before Christmas, I called each of them and let them know of our plans. They were surprised, but understood. They wished us well and made arrangements to come by and deliver presents a few days before we were to leave Denver for Southern California.

We were getting excited about our trip. We had never been to Disneyland and neither had our kids. It was just one of those things we never got around to doing. Since we planned on staying a week and going on every ride at least once, we decided to rent a small home along the coast.

The day of our trip arrived. It was three days before Christmas. "Mike, are we doing the right thing leaving the kids at Christmas and going somewhere that we promised them we would take them and never did?"

"Maggie, how old are the kids?" It was a question that needed no answer and that answered her question at the same time.

"I know, but I wish they were going with us."

"This is our time. Let's enjoy it without thinking of the kids. They'll be just fine."

The next two days were the best days of our lives. We laughed and ate until our stomachs hurt. We decided to not go to Disneyland on Christmas Day, but to simply be with each other, take out some DVDs we'd brought, watch *It's a Wonderful Life, A Christmas Story*, and the Disney animated version of *A Christmas Carol.*

Maggie made French toast for breakfast with freshly squeezed orange juice and coffee. It was like we were in heaven. She had planned to cook our Christmas dinner later in the afternoon. The kitchen was small, but adequate for the two of us.

"So, what's on the menu for tonight? Any hints as to the special Christmas dish?" I was fishing, but she wasn't biting. I'd get no help from her.

"You'll just have to wait and see. I hope you'll like it." She went back into the kitchen and I turned on the TV to watch some basketball.

Here we were, after fifty years of marriage, back to the same Christmas as our first, alone just the two of us.

Maggie put the dinner in the oven, came over to the couch, and snuggled in my arms. We kissed and remembered that first Christmas so many years ago. I turned off the basketball game and we dozed in each other's arms.

Around 4:00, there was a knock at the door. We had decided to not answer it. It couldn't be for us. A minute later, another knock, but this time a little louder.

"For crying out loud! Don't people have anything better to do than to bother people they don't know on Christmas Day?"

"Now, Mike, maybe there's something wrong with the car or something. Just go see who it is then we'll continue our nap. Dinner won't be ready until around 6:00."

I got up and made my way to the door in the middle of some more rapping. "I'm coming, I'm coming!" I yelled.

I got to the door, unlocked it, opened it, and there on the porch were boxes and boxes of food. I looked around, but couldn't see anyone. I thought that they must have the wrong house, but there was no one around to return it to so I just brought it into the kitchen.

"Who was it?" Maggie asked from the living room.

"I don't know. There were three boxes of food on the porch. It's as if someone thought that we needed food for Christmas dinner. Strange."

We had just gotten settled back onto the couch when there was another knock at the door. It made sense. Someone figured out that they had left the food at the wrong address. I was not prepared for what happened next.

I got to the door, opened it, and from all sides of the house came a coordinated cry, "SURPRISE!"

It was the kids with all of their kids, about fifteen in all.

"What are you doing here?" Maggie came running to the door, tears streaming down her face. I was both elated and confused.

Jamie, our eldest, spoke for the tribe. "When you told us that you were not going to be home for Christmas, we thought that we had done something to make you not want to be home with us."

"No, no, nothing like that," Maggie and I blurted almost simultaneously.

"Then John told us about last Christmas and how we all were so insensitive to your needs while taking care of our own. Mom and Dad, we owe you so much. We just couldn't be without you on Christmas this year." They all hugged, kissed, and moved into the living room.

Then, one of our grandkids, I don't know which one, spoke the truth as only kids can understand it, "Of course, it didn't hurt that you were here in sunny California going to Disneyland." We all laughed.

The grandkids brought several computers to play games on, the girls went into the kitchen to whip up a quick, but delicious Christmas dinner for all of us, and us guys did what we always do; watch basketball and football.

When dinner was finished and plans made to go to Disneyland the next day, the kids packed up their families, kissed us goodbye, and took off for their hotel, but not before Joan gave us a very special Christmas gift. It was a cookbook with all of the families' special Christmas recipes in it. Maggie's picture in a Santa hat was on the cover titled, *A Special Christmas Tradition.*

As great as the cookbook was, there is no way to describe the gift that our kids gave to us that Christmas Day. Needless to say, it was the best gift of all; the gift of family love.

Day Six
The Cause for Claus

Well, it's been fun while it lasted and it lasted a good long time, but now it's over. At least I think it's over. No, I'm sure it's over. How could I have been so stupid to play along for as long as I did? I want it to be over. Yes, it's definitely over.

Here I am at 65 years old and just now letting go of my childish obsession with Santa Claus. Every year for the past forty years, I've been an agent in the "Cause for Claus." Every year, without fail, I compared myself to Jolly Old St. Nick. I grew the beard, whitened it, rouged my cheeks, and spent hours a day sitting in the most uncomfortable chairs. Oh, they looked big and comfortable, but you sit for hours at a time with kids jumping up and down on your lap and see how comfortable that chair is then.

Don't get me wrong, it wasn't all terrible. It couldn't have been, for me to have done it for forty years. Well, maybe it was terrible and I just didn't want to admit it. Anyway, it's now definitely over. I got a call today from Macy's wanting to set my schedule for the Thanksgiving – Christmas season. Needless to say, Mr. Harmon was shocked to hear that I wouldn't be coming back.

"Jim, you've got to be kidding!" He practically yelled into the phone. "Is it the money? We can discuss that if it is. You've been the best Santa Macy's has ever had. C'mon, Jim, tell me. What's it gonna take?"

I wasn't expecting Mr. Harmon to beg me to come back. I was especially surprised by his statement that I had been their best Santa. I guess you could say that because I was their only Santa. Well, almost. There was the guy I replaced in their first season forty years ago. He just wasn't cutting it. He showed up late nearly every day, didn't particularly like kids, and did practically nothing to invite customers to buy at Macy's what Little Johnny or Janie wanted.

I noticed what was going on when we took our own kids to visit Santa at the new Macy's. I've never been one to complain, but I just couldn't let 'Uncaring Santa' spoil the image of the store that was supposed to turn the shopping mall into a tax cash cow; to say nothing of the experience my girls, Martha and Evelyn, would have. I left them with Nancy to do some Christmas shopping and I found a manager who directed me to the Personnel Office on the third floor.

As I walked through the aisles of quality goods decked out in holiday cheer to get to the escalator, it dawned on me that, while I was instrumental in bringing Macy's to Manchester, I really didn't know why their prices had to be higher than everyone else in town. Quite honestly, this was my first time in Macy's.

As the youngest member of the City Council, I made my decision to support bringing Macy's to the city purely on the taxes and jobs that would be created by having a major department store in our small east-end mall. I felt that

I had put my Masters in Public Administration to good use. Now what I wanted to see was a thriving business. So, it just made sense that I should take up the situation of the 'Uncaring Santa' with someone who could affect a change.

Even though this was my first time in this new Macy's, I was pretty sure that Santa wasn't going to get any better. I had heard stories from our neighbors. When I reached the Personnel Office, I told the girl at the receptionist's desk what my problem was and she began directing me to Customer Service. I could see a pattern forming here. I was not going to be shunted from department to department until I gave up.

"You don't understand, Miss. I want to see your Personnel Director," I stated quite forcefully.

"I'll see if he's in." She disappeared into the Director's office and came back stating that Mr. Harmon was busy, but would be happy to speak with me in a half hour or so. I was directed to a comfortable chair across from the door.

Exactly one half hour after I sat down, Mr. Harmon rolled out of his office. I was surprised to meet a man practically my own age. As I would find out, he was one of the Macy's Wiz Kids who was hired directly out of college with his MBA to run the Personnel Department of the Manchester Macy's. He had apprenticed in Bedford before being assigned to this store.

"What can I do for you, sir?" asked Mr. Harmon. "I'm sorry that you had to wait."

I could tell that he really meant it. "How do you do, Mr. Harmon? I know that your time is valuable so I'll get right to my issue."

"Let me save you some time," he cut me off. "You have an issue with our Santa and your concern is for both your girls and our customers in general. Did I get it right?"

He waited for me to confirm which I did.

"We here at Macy's take complaints about our employees very seriously. We know that negative comments to friends, family, and neighbors are a prescription for ultimate failure. I pride myself on responding to each complaint personally. I assure you that Santa will be dealt with before the day is out. Is there anything else?"

What could I say? He took on my issue and made it his. What more could I expect? I trusted that he would do what he said he'd do. "Thank you very much. It's been a pleasure meeting with a true professional. I look forward to shopping in your store and telling my friends about your concern for their experience here at Macy's," I said.

Mr. Harmon extended his hand and wished me and my family a Merry Christmas. I collected Nancy and the girls and shared my experience with her on the way home.

"What makes you think that he's going to do anything at all?" she questioned. "I mean, what's his incentive to follow up? He did what a good manager is supposed to do. He got rid of the complaint. He sounds like he's very good at his job, but, really, do you honestly think that he's going to do anything about Santa? Be honest." Nancy got her Bachelor's Degree in Marketing and was a whiz when it came to making things happen.

"So, what would you have done differently? I thought I did pretty well," I stated.

"It sounds good for what it was, but you left out the most important step in effecting change."

Now she was starting to get on my nerves. "What exactly was *that,* Madame Marketing Director?"

"You don't have to get snippy with me. I'm just trying to help."

"Okay, okay. I'm sorry. What did I forget?" I learned long ago not to match wits with her. It's not that she was always right, but that's how it always ended up, if you know what I mean.

She looked at me with those disapproving eyes. "You didn't request confirmation of his effort. If he's as 'enlightened' as you think, then he should have no problem letting you know what he has done to rectify the situation."

"Don't you think that's information best held between the employee and Mr. Harmon? How would you feel if one of your clients became privileged to know what you and your boss had discussed about your performance? I'm sure that there's some law that protects the rights of the employee in this regard."

She thought about it a bit and finally agreed with my assessment. "I'm sure you're right, but that doesn't mean that you couldn't check in next week to see how our Santa is doing."

"Very good idea, my dear. Now, what's for dinner?"

I hadn't had any great relationship with Santa Claus when I was growing up. Our family wasn't that well off so his identity was given to me early so as not to have very high expectations of presents under the tree. I wasn't greedy or anything like that, but up until I knew the *truth*, I always thought that I had not been as good as I could be. Finally, around seven or eight, I just gave up trying and even started to cause trouble just to prove my point. It got so bad that my teacher started calling home at least once a week with everything from missing assignments to backtalk. Who knew that Santa could cause so much trouble in a kid's life?

Well, once I knew that Mom and Dad provided us with our meager Christmas, I straightened out and started getting good grades again while staying out of trouble. It was at this time in my life that I recognized what it meant to be poor. Until then, I was perfectly content to live with my two brothers and sister in a house that soon grew too small for all of us siblings to sleep in the same room.

It was hard being the eldest, knowing the 'Santa Secret' and not being able to share it with my younger siblings. The only saving grace of being the only one to know was that Mom treated me extra nice at Christmas time. I mean, she always treated us kids nice, but at Christmas I would get an extra cookie or a larger piece of Mom's famous pecan pie or a sweet here and there. We never talked about it, but I knew why I was getting the "extras."

Then one year, it didn't matter anymore. I was twelve and my brothers and sister were nine, eight, and seven. It was a snowy mid-December night. It had been snowing for three days straight. The yard was covered in a blanket of white. The sidewalks were icy and we couldn't even go out to make a snowman or sled down Somerville Street.

Dad had stayed home from work all three days to make sure that the pipes didn't burst and to keep wood in the fireplace. There was no school for us because of the weather so we got to stay up late. We had just finished decorating the tree and were sitting all together drinking hot cocoa and eating Christmas cookies that Mom had baked that afternoon when the phone rang.

We wondered who it could be at 10:00 at night. Dad answered. It was his boss telling him that he had to be at work for the midnight shift or lose his job. I suppose that Mom could have taken care of the pipes, but Dad wanted to make sure that we were all taken care of. He argued with his boss, but finally Mom convinced him that we would be alright and that he should go if he felt he could get to the train yards without any trouble.

My dad worked really hard and was intent on making a better life for his family. He was being considered for a foreman's job. Besides working 40 hours a week plus overtime, he worked at an ice cream parlor on the weekends. He was the best worker on his crew so it hurt him that his boss threatened him with firing if he didn't show up to help unload the five boxcars of cement that had just pulled into the yard.

I'll never forget that December Friday night. Dad bundled up with two shirts, a heavy jacket, scarf, gloves, hat, and galoshes. It was nearly 20 degrees out and still snowing heavily. He said that he'd be fine. We all got together in a group hug and sent him on his way. Mom, clutching her bathrobe to her chin, went out on the porch to see him off. The last memory I have of my father was him blowing Mom a kiss and my mom catching it.

After Dad left, we finished our cocoa and went to bed. I think that it was around 12:30 when there came a heavy knock at the door. Mom got up and so did I. She turned on the light in the living room. I watched from our bedroom door not sure what to expect.

Mom turned on the porch light and looked out through the window in the door. I saw her take a step back and put a hand to her mouth as though stifling a scream. She unlocked the door and opened it.

"Mrs. James Morgan?" the taller of the two Bedford police officers asked.

"Yes, what's happened? Please tell me." I could see her shaking so I went to her.

"Mom, what's the matter? Is it Dad?"

"I'm sorry Mrs. Morgan, but your husband has been in an accident."

Mom pulled me close to her. "How bad is it, Officer? He's alright, isn't he?"

The two officers looked at each other and the shorter of the two answered. "He rolled his car about two miles from here as he was trying to negotiate a turn. The car went over an embankment and plunged into the river. A passing motorist saw the whole thing and did everything he could to save your husband, but there really was nothing that he could do."

Mom fell to the ground. "No!" she screamed. "No, it's not true. There must be something that can be done," she yelled.

I didn't say a word. It was all too horrible to comprehend. Hadn't we just been decorating the tree and having cocoa together as a family? Hadn't my dad done what he thought was the right thing by going in to work? Why did my mom have to push him to go to work tonight? That last question made me sick to my stomach. How could I even think of blaming my mom for the accident?

I held her tight and we both cried. One of the officers bent down and asked if there was anyone we'd like to call. Through her continual sobbing she said that she wanted to call Grandpa Morgan to come over to be with us.

The officers got the number and made the call for us. Grandpa was not in much better shape than Mom when he arrived. The officers said that they would be removing the car in the morning at first light and would let us know when we could get Dad's body to make arrangements.

When I heard this, a thought flashed through my mind. "Wait a minute? How do you know that was my dad in the car? Are you sure it's even his car?"

Officer Slade put his hands on my shoulders, "Son, even though we couldn't get to the car last night, we were able to see the plates and that's how we got to you. Do you understand?"

I did and that glimmer of hope receded back into the darkness.

Mom finally fell asleep on the couch around 6:00 a.m. Grandpa and I went into the kitchen and just sat at the table.

"Grandpa, why did God take my dad? He was always praying and he made sure that we all went to Church every Sunday. Why does God want someone good like that? Does He think that Dad's work on earth is done?" I asked a lot of questions without really expecting much of an answer.

Grandpa folded his hands as if in prayer and looked at the crucifix hanging over the door leading into the living room before looking me straight in the eyes. "That's not an easy question to answer, Jim. Your dad was a good man, and I don't say that because he was my son, but because he always looked out for others. If he had a dollar and somebody needed it, he would give it to him without a second thought. He always knew that his reward would come when he met God in heaven. But, I'm pretty sure that he didn't think that he would be meeting Him so soon, though. None of us know when we will be called to account for ourselves before God. We just have to be prepared."

"That seems easier said than done, Grandpa." I wasn't sure why he wasn't more upset. It's like he had accepted God's will and wasn't angry with Him. Maybe that was it. By putting his trust in God, Grandpa could accept that his only son was gone. I wished that I had that same kind of faith, but why should I? I was only twelve.

It was getting light out and the kids would be up soon. How was Mom going to tell them? I walked into the living room where Mom was still sleeping on the couch. Grandpa was getting his jacket on along with his boots, hat, scarf, and gloves.

"Where are you going, Grandpa? Can I go?" Now that Dad was gone, I would have to be the man of the family and I needed lessons. Grandpa would be the perfect teacher.

"I'm heading out to watch the police bring up your father's car. I don't think that you should go. I don't know what we'll find. You stay here and tell your mom that I'll be back as soon as I can. I have to check in on your grandma. I haven't told her yet."

I didn't envy Grandpa having to tell Grandma. Dad was their only child and I'm sure that neither of them ever thought that they'd be burying him before they died. I heard Mom scurrying about in the living room. She went to the bathroom and stayed there for a good long time. I could hear her crying again.

I went back into the kitchen and plugged in the pot of coffee that Mom had put together for Dad when he came home after his midnight shift. I didn't much like coffee, but I figured that I'd better start getting used to it now that I was the man of the house.

Mom came out of the bathroom and asked where Grandpa was. I told her, and she started crying again, mumbling that it should have been her. At first, I thought that she was talking about the accident, but after listening to her for a while, it was obvious that she was saying that it should have been her who went to the river to watch the police take out the car with my dad in it.

"Mom, the kids will be up soon. I think they'll need us to be strong. What can I do to help?" I had always been more mature than my years would allow.

Mom held me close, mussed my hair, and kissed my forehead. "My little man," she said. "Life will be different now. We'll all have to pull together to make it. Your dad was the only breadwinner of our family. I'm going to have to go to work. You'll have to take care of your brothers and sister. I know that it's not fair to you, but there's not much else we can do. I'm sure that Grandpa and Grandma will help from time to time, but we can't rely on others until we do all that we can to provide for ourselves."

I spent just a moment taking it all in. I said, "I understand, Mom. I love you."

Tears appeared in the corners of her eyes again and she said, "I love you, too."

The funeral was on a clear but cold December 20th in the only Catholic Church in Bedford, New Hampshire. The church was filled with friends and family. Some had travelled completely across country to be with Mom and us along with Grandpa and Grandma. My dad was well-respected among the community so practically everyone was there. The Mass was beautiful. The choir sang his favorite song, "Ave Maria." There was not a dry eye in the church. We buried him in the local cemetery and left him to be alone for Christmas, but not before we placed a huge Christmas wreath on his plot to tell him how much we loved him.

It had been an emotional day for all of us when I suddenly remembered that Christmas was only five days away. I hadn't done any shopping and I was sure that the kids hadn't done any either. Maybe shopping for each other would help us to get over the loss of our father. Mom was in the kitchen cleaning up after the wake. Grandma was drying the dishes that Mom had washed. My cousin Maggie was cleaning off the table and other relatives were helping where they could.

I wandered into the kitchen. "Mom, please don't take this wrong, but what do you think about going on a small Christmas shopping trip with the kids tomorrow to maybe help them get over Dad's death? We've all saved our allowances to buy each other presents. What do you think?"

Mom and Grandma exchanged glances. It was Grandma that spoke. "Jim, I think that's a wonderful idea. I have some shopping of my own to do tomorrow, how about if you all join me?"

I saw Mom wipe a tear away from her eye with her apron. "Is that okay, Mom?" I asked.

"That would be fine. I'm sure that your dad would approve. Thanks for thinking about your brothers and sister.

They need you right now and I can tell that you're prepared to be responsible for them. I wish that you didn't have to be, but you'll never know how much this means to me. I love you, son." She gave me a big hug and a kiss on the head.

"Me, too," Grandma said and gave me another kiss and hug.

The next day, we got up, brushed our teeth, ate breakfast, and got dressed like we usually did. I gathered the kids and told them the good news that Grandma would be picking us up around 10:00 to go Christmas shopping for each other. You should have heard the squeals. You would have thought that they had just won a lottery or something.

We each went to our own secret hiding place where we kept our money. We didn't have much, but it was honest earned and it felt good to be able to spend our own money instead of being given money to buy Christmas presents. Grandma showed up right on time.

"You kids ready to go?" she asked with a smile in her voice.

As if in unison, all of us screeched, "Yeah! Let's go!" We put on our jackets, kissed Mom, and led Grandma out the door.

"Don't wait on us for lunch, honey. I'm taking the kids out." More screeching. We ran to the car almost slipping on the icy sidewalk. I called 'shotgun' and the other three piled into the backseat.

"Everyone set to go?" Grandma asked. There were no negatives so off we went to Macy's to go shopping. Little did I know how that one shopping trip would change my life.

We got to Macy's and went straight to the toy department. Grandma took Joan and Jack, the two youngest. Harry came with me. We tried to stay in different aisles so that no one could see what the other was buying for them. When we had finished our shopping, Grandma said that she had a surprise for us before we went to lunch.

What kid doesn't like surprises? "What?" we all barked.

"Follow me." We did, and what a surprise it turned out to be – for some of us.

The sign read, "Line up here for your visit with Santa Claus." I was pretty sure that Joan and Jack still believed, but I wasn't sure about Harry. I knew where I stood on the whole Santa Claus thing so I had to be careful not to let the cat out of the bag. The line wasn't too long so I was sure that we would be done in no time then off to lunch.

I was right. First Joan, then Jack, and Harry jumped up on the jolly old elf's lap. As I was walking out of the line, Joan tugged at my coat. "Aren't you going to tell Santa what you want for Christmas, Jim?"

How could I tell her what I knew to be the truth? So, I climbed the few stairs to Santa's lap. "Santa, I'm just doing this 'coz my brothers and sister still believe in you, but I don't. I know that you're just some guy hired by the store to sell toys so can we just make this short?"

"Who told you such a story, Jim? Never mind, I know. It had to be an adult. It's a shame that adults don't remember the magic of their first few Christmases. Can you remember back that far?"

I couldn't believe that this guy was actually trying to change my thoughts about Santa. I could remember, but I didn't want to waste any more time. I was hungry. "It's okay, Santa, or whoever you are. I've been here long enough for my family to believe that I asked for something for Christmas. Nice try on getting me to believe in you again." With that, I got off his lap and started down the stairs. Then it dawned on me – how did he know my name? One of the kids must have told him. When I turned around to ask him, he was gone. All that was near his chair was a sign stating that Santa had to go feed his reindeer and would be back in an hour. I was a little confused, but just chalked it all up to poor timing. He must have been scheduled to go to lunch right at that time.

We only had to wait a little while for Grandma to return from her own little shopping spree. "Did everybody talk to Santa? Did you tell him what you want for Christmas?" The kids all nodded their heads and spilled their guts – a doll for Joanie, a spaceship for Jack, and a BB gun for Harry. "What about you, Jim? What did you ask Santa to bring you this Christmas?"

I didn't want to lie to Grandma, but I couldn't really tell her the truth with the kids around. "Well, I don't want to tell. I think that if you tell, you won't get it. So, I'm gonna keep it a secret." Joanie began to cry.

"What's the matter, honey?" Grandma asked blotting her tears with a tissue.

"I told, so now I won't get my doll," she blurted.

"Oh, Joanie, that's just what Jim believes. There are plenty of children who tell what they want and still get what they asked for. Don't worry. You told Santa and he has you on his list. Now, who's hungry?"

I was glad that Grandma changed the subject. We left Macy's carrying our bundles, filled the trunk, and piled back into the car.

"Where are we going for lunch, Grandma?" Harry asked.

"Well, it's not a fancy place, but they make the best hot fudge sundaes in the city. If you eat all your lunch, maybe you'll get one if you aren't too full."

"Do I get my own or do I have to share?" Joanie wondered.

Grandma knew that the sundaes were pretty big so she was expecting to share with both of the little ones. "We'll see," she said diplomatically.

I was kinda surprised where Grandma took us for lunch. It was F.W. Woolworth. We sat at the counter and watched the cook prepare our sandwiches. I wanted a hamburger, but Grandma insisted that we all just have sandwiches. To this day, I still don't know why. We all finished our lunch, then came the most wonderful hot fudge sundae there ever was. We gobbled them down and slowly made our way back to the car. Our stomachs were so bloated with gooey marshmallow and sticky hot fudge that we could hardly walk.

We got home and took our presents to different rooms to wrap them in secret, but not before thanking Grandma with hugs and kisses.

"That was really good for them. I took them to see Santa and I got their lists. The only one I didn't get was Jim's. He wouldn't tell me what he asked for."

"He actually saw Santa? That's amazing. Even though he saw Santa, I'm pretty sure that he didn't ask for anything.

We had to tell him a few years ago that there was no Santa. It was affecting his grades and behavior. Don't ask. It's a long story. I'll tell you later."

"Alright... so, if you had to guess, what would you say he'd like for Christmas?" Grandma probed.

Mom thought for a while and finally said, "You know, he fancies himself a writer so maybe some writing books and pens or pencils."

"Really? You think he'd like that?"

"I'm pretty sure. I know it's not much, but he's a pretty frugal boy when it comes to expenditures. I think that it all comes from when we had to tell him how poor we really were. It was right around the time that we had to tell him about Santa.

"Thanks, Mom, for taking the kids out today. I'm pretty sure that it was the right thing to do. I know it was better than just sitting around the house thinking about their dad."

The next four days were filled with sledding, snowball fights, visiting friends, and getting ready for Christmas Eve and Christmas Day. I had heard Mom and Grandma talking so I was pretty sure what I was getting. It was true that I did like to write, but that's not quite what I asked for in my heart as I sat on Santa's lap. I don't know why I asked for anything, but I did. If I don't believe in Santa, why would I believe that he could read my mind? Maybe it was the fact that he tried to get me to believe in him again. Plus, there was just something about him that seemed so familiar. Who knows, maybe I saw him when I was a kid.

So, it was here – Christmas Eve. Early to bed was the order of the day so that Santa didn't miss our house. Mom had baked some Christmas cookies earlier in the day so we left some out for him. Joanie and Jack even left some carrots for the reindeer.

Christmas morning always began around 6:00 when the kids got up and made their way downstairs to see what Santa brought. Mom was already up napping on the couch. She and Dad used to be there together. It would be different this year and every year thereafter.

What a surprise! Joanie got a doll, Jack got a spaceship, and Harry didn't get a BB gun, but he did get an air rifle – less chance of "putting his eye out." When it came time for me to open my gifts, I was surprised that I had two packages – one from Grandpa and Grandma and another from Santa. Grandma and Grandpa did give me writing paper and pens. I hesitated to open the other package. I looked at Mom and all she said was, "Open it." So I did.

Tears began streaming down my face. There in the box was Dad's Boy Scout knife. He told me when we were on a campout once that I would get his knife when he was finished with it. Dad was our Troop Leader and he made camping so much fun. We always learned something new at each campout. How did Mom know that, in my heart, I had asked Santa for the knife.

I wiped the tears on my pajama sleeve. "Mom, did Dad tell you to give me his knife? He told me that he'd give it to me when he was finished with it, but I never thought I'd see it again. I didn't know where it was."

Mom just looked at the knife. "I didn't give that to you, Jim. Are you sure that there wasn't another label on it saying who it was from?"

I searched the mounds of paper, but found no tag. Could it be? Was there really a Santa Claus? How else could I explain it? No one owned up to finding it and giving it to me.

As sad as that Christmas Day was without Dad, the gift I received from my 'secret' Santa set me on a path to become an Eagle Scout and to seek leadership roles in my work and my community.

Now you know what Santa has meant to me in my life and it's time to get back to my most recent encounter with him. If you remember, I had just told Mr. Harmon that I was done portraying Santa after forty years at Macy's, and as Paul Harvey used to say, "And now… the rest of the story."

I met with Mr. Harmon and explained to him that I was just plain worn out of playing Santa. He understood, but still needed a Santa. I recommended my best friend's son, Mike. He applied and got the job which was good because he had been out of work for several months.

One day in early December, I stopped in to speak with Mr. Harmon to see how Mike was doing. "He's doing just great. He has a way with kids and adults," he said. "We may keep him on in our toy department after Christmas."

"That would be great. He should be good with kids, he's got six of his own," I responded. "I think it's nice that we keep it in the family. What do you think?"

"I couldn't agree with you more. One of the best decisions I ever made was hiring you to replace 'Uncaring Santa' as you used to call him.

"What are you going to do now that you're not playing Santa?"

"I've been giving that some thought and I think that I'll unpack the suit and wear it again."

"What? Why did you quit if you're still going to play Santa? You're not going to Penny's, are you?" he stammered.

"No, no, nothing like that. I was at the Veteran's Hospital visiting a friend when I overheard the nurse on the floor telling her supervisor that they were going to have to cancel the kids Christmas party because they couldn't find a Santa. Well, you know me. I up and volunteered that very minute. When I told her that I had been the Macy's Santa for forty years, she began to blush and giggle."

"Why do you suppose she did that? Let me guess. She sat on your lap when she was just a girl. Am I right?"

"You are, but not only her. There were about fifteen nurses and doctors on that one floor alone that claim to have sat on Santa's lap at Macy's. I can't tell you how it made me feel when they all gathered around and shared their memories of Christmas's past."

"Well, Santa, it looks like you made a difference in a lot of people's lives."

"I suppose I have and I owe it all to that Christmas when my dad died. To this day, I have no idea how Santa knew that I wanted my dad's Boy Scout knife."

"Great-grandma, I'm here. Which couch do you need moved?" Everyone called my mom great-grandma. Mike bent over and gave her a kiss on the cheek.

"That one over there," she said in a feeble voice. She had lived in that same house practically her entire life. It was the same house that we lived in as kids.

"Where do you want it?" Mike asked. I knew what came next. "Jim, can you give me a hand?"

What could I say, "Of course. Which end?"

After we moved the couch, she asked, "Are you still going to have your Christmas Eve party?"

"We're planning on it. You're coming, right?"

"If it's not too cold out. You know how easily I catch bronchitis at this time of year."

It's true that she caught bronchitis easily, but I'm pretty sure that she used that excuse almost every year to get out of coming to the Christmas Eve party. I think that she just wanted to be alone with her memories of us kids growing up with her and Dad.

Just before Mike started up the vacuum to hoover the rug that had lain under the couch for eons, he spotted some paper that looked too big to be sucked into the vacuum. Just as he was about to ball it up and throw it away, he noticed the writing. He couldn't believe his eyes.

"Jim, look at this. What do you make of it?" Mike shared the scrap of Christmas wrapping paper with me.

"That's amazing!" I couldn't believe my eyes.

"What did you find, Jim? Is it valuable?" Mom asked with curiosity.

"Maybe. It answers a question from that first Christmas without Dad. Here, read it."

"I can't. I don't have my glasses. You read it to me."

"Okay," I began to read. "'Merry Christmas, Jim. Please take care of my knife. I'll love you always.'" It was simply signed, "Dad."

Day Seven
The Christmas Kiss

So here it is early morning Christmas Eve and I still don't have anything down on paper. Why do I always wait and hope that the 'spirit' will provide me with a storyline that will entertain my family at Christmas? Maybe because that seems to be the way it works with me.

I've tried to write my Christmas story during the year, but I just can't seem to work on anything unless I'm under the gun, so to speak. This year is no different. I've been thinking about a particular storyline, but I can't seem to get to the point where I have a clear picture of the beginning, middle, and end. Maybe I should just begin and let the characters take me where they will. Well, here goes. There's no time left to do anything else. No dialogue this year, just first-person narrative. Enjoy!

For some strange reason, I've always considered the moon a personal friend of mine. Sounds strange, but it's true. Ever since I was a little boy I've been fascinated by the moon. I've sat gazing at it for hours at a time, just wondering why I had a special connection to it.

When I was little, it was that I was interested in the different shapes that the moon would make in the sky each night. How did it do that, I wondered. Then as I grew older and I learned something about science, I came to understand that the moon took different shapes because of where it was behind the earth with the sun on the other side of the earth. It actually was the sun's reflection off the moon's surface. What an 'enlightening' experience!

I was sixteen when my fascination with the moon began to wane. You could say that something else took over my passion for moon gazing. Monica was the same age as me and I had been smitten by her since fourth grade in Sister Angelica's class. Her eyes were as blue as polar ice. Her hair, the color of yellow corn. She always had a smile on her face and a kind word to say of just about anyone. She could sing, too, which made her all the more intriguing to me. I've always thought of people with talent as lucky people because they could make others happy with their talent. She certainly made me happy with her singing. She even encouraged me to join the church choir when I had a hard time just staying on pitch. I didn't really want to, but I did it for her and to be near her.

There was no other girl for me. We went everywhere together. Now that was tough seeing as how we went to different high schools and I didn't drive. Back then, it was no big thing to ask your dad to drive you on a date. I guess it still happens, but now kids see it as parents intruding into their lives or some such nonsense. Anyway, that's a story for a different time.

While I thought highly of Monica from fourth grade on, I didn't think of her as my girlfriend until my sixteenth birthday. That was the day of my first kiss. On a scale of 1 to 10, you could probably call it a two, but it was everything to me and her. It was also her first kiss.

My parents had thrown me a surprise sixteenth birthday party with all of my friends there. I'm sure there had been other parties, but this was the only one I can remember. I had friends there from my Scout Troop, my family, school, and the Church Youth Group. Monica and I were officers in the Youth Group so we had to get together before each meeting to plan the evening and discuss the events that we wanted to put together for the rest of the kids.

The most fun projects we would work on were the dances. There weren't DJs back in the day so we would have either live bands if we could afford them or someone would play their records – that's right, vinyl records; no cassettes, CDs, or MP3 players. It didn't matter. All we cared about was being together as a group.

Getting back to the birthday party. I don't remember what I got from anyone else except Monica. She gave me the newest LP from "The New Christy Minstrels." As I mentioned, she was into music and she was nurturing what she perceived as an interest in me for music. I think I still have that record around somewhere.

Mom and Dad had moved the couch, chair, and coffee table to the walls and my little brother pretended that he was Dick Clark and 'spun the platters' for us to all dance to. He would even give each song a dance rating. Even though the intent was for us to dance, we were all too shy. Visualize if you will, about fifteen kids all standing around tapping toes, snapping fingers, singing along, but not a one dancing. It wasn't for lack of encouragement by my parents.

The clock had just gonged 10:00 p.m. and the party was about over. Parents started showing up to pick up kids and that's when it happened. One of my best friends started ragging on me that I was "sweet 16 and never been kissed." All my friends knew that I liked Monica above all others of her kind. They wanted to see me kiss or be kissed. The truth was that I was "sweet 16 and never been kissed."

Being a very shy boy, I didn't know quite how to respond to their jabs. Monica really wasn't helping by staying near the table with all the opened gifts on it. I couldn't decide if I should give her a peck on the cheek or really go for it and kiss her on the lips or do nothing at all. What was a boy to do? Luckily, I didn't have to think about it too long. The rest of the parents showed up and rescued me from my torture. I could tell that Monica was relieved also.

After all had gone, my dad and I took Monica home. She lived on the other side of town so it would take about fifteen minutes to get her home. On the way there, we reviewed the evening and even tried to sing one of the "New Christy Minstrels'" songs. It was "Green, Green," I think.

Even though it was early spring, the weather had turned cool and damp. As I walked Monica to the door, our hands brushed each other and, for some unexplained reason, I wrapped my hand around hers and we walked hand-in-hand to the door, neither of us speaking.

The porch light was on and we could hear the TV blaring in the living room. Her father was hard of hearing. I was just about to say good night when I noticed the moon. It was as though my heart skipped a beat. It shone big, full, and beautiful. I turned to Monica and told her of my passion for the moon. I'm sure she thought I was loony, but being the polite person that she was, she listened and told me that she thought I was a romantic. I wasn't quite sure what that was, but if it came from her, I was sure that it was a good thing.

For a few moments we just stood holding hands on the porch looking at the moon. No words were necessary. Our hands softly explored each other's and, as if on cue, we turned and kissed. Not a strong passionate kiss, but a tender soft kiss that I remember to this day. The moon has never been as bright as on that evening.

As things happen in life, after high school, Monica and I sort of drifted apart. She wanted one thing that took her away to school and I wanted something else that kept me home. We tried to work on our relationship from a distance, but it soon proved to be impossible. After some time, we agreed to separate. It was not an easy thing to do, and at the time, I wasn't sure that it was the right thing to do. I loved her and I think she loved me. We never said the words so I guess you could say that neither of us had invested what was required to keep the relationship alive.

Monica received her bachelor's degree in early childhood development and went to work as a teacher. During our college years, I'd keep in touch with her through her family. I'd stop over every once in a while to get the news. It seemed better to get first-hand information rather than waiting for her to come home. I wrote letters, but that soon became a challenge as each of us had classes to study for and papers to write. After the first year, there were no more letters either way.

I wasn't able to finish my degree in Native American Anthropology. I just couldn't concentrate. Mid-way through my sophomore year, a friend of mine from Scouts stopped by the house and luckily caught me home. Roger had joined the Air Force and told me all about the great programs they had. Just out of curiosity, I went in to talk to a recruiter. I was nineteen and the Vietnam War was raging.

Joining the Air Force helped take my mind off of Monica, but she was still never far away. I really didn't want to get rid of the memory of the good times we had had since my sixteenth birthday and my first kiss. As we agreed, I dated other girls, but I felt as though I was betraying a trust. It would take a long time for that feeling to go away. In fact, it never went away until I met Bonnie.

Bonnie turned out to be the new light of my life. For as much as I thought I loved Monica, I experienced that same level of love with Bonnie. We got married while I was overseas and made a wonderful life together having three beautiful children. I finally finished school and went to work for the State of California's IPPP (Indigenous Peoples Preservation Program).

Bonnie and I were cut from the same cloth. We supported our kids in anything and everything they wanted to do. Mick became a doctor, Jackie an artist, and we were still trying to figure out what Simon, our twenty-one-year-old wanted to be, when Bonnie got sick. It was the hardest time of our lives. At first, it was just a cough that wouldn't go away. It never got better and then the fever came. She had chills and sweats at the same time. I called Mick and he had his mother driven by ambulance to the emergency room at Juniper Hospital where he met us.

She was immediately placed in a quarantined room and in intensive care. Mick assured us that it was just precautionary, but there were several other people in the quarantined room. Needless to say, we were all worried. Jackie flew in from New York and Simon came home from his trip to the South Seas. Jackie made it. Simon didn't. Bonnie died just thirty hours after having been admitted.

The doctors knew what she had when they looked at her on admission. They had just seen three other cases. One had died and the other two were in the room that Bonnie was put into. No one, not even Mick, could have known that Bonnie had been infected with the rarest of diseases that kills about half of those infected.

The children were devastated, especially Simon who could not be found in time. He was out on a boat island hopping when he got the word that his mother had died. He flew home as soon as he could. He landed hours before the funeral, just having time to shower, change, and pay his own personal final respects to the mother that he loved so dearly. Of all the kids, Simon was always her baby. Mick and Jackie matured early in life. They both knew exactly what they wanted to do and they pursued their goals with all that was in them until they achieved the success that they craved.

Simon, on the other hand, had a hard time figuring it out. He was probably the brightest of the three kids, but never really applied himself to the task of learning. He played football, basketball, and golf. Sports seemed to be enough for him. Because he was so bright, he was able to make do with his education and got by with a smattering of 'A's', some 'B's' and way too many 'C's'. His grades weren't good enough to get him into a Division I university and, while he was first string at each of the sports that he played, he wasn't good enough to earn a scholarship anywhere.

While Simon tried this and that, he wasn't ever really great at anything. Bonnie always thought that greatness lay just ahead of him in something. She didn't know what, but she knew that it would just be a matter of time before his light shone brightly to illuminate the darkness somewhere. She would not be wrong.

Simon was so affected by his mother's death that he settled back into the family home and proceeded to go to school. He had found his goal and would not be moved from it. Simon would become a doctor and go into research to find a cure for what had killed his mother.

I was satisfied with the kids and their chosen professions. Bonnie would be proud of them and their children. I really enjoyed being 'Grandpa' and taking the kids on summer vacations to the lake that our own family had spent so many happy summers on. We'd boat, swim, fish, and just have a great time playing games all day – no TV, no telephone, no anything to get in the way of grandfather and grandkids bonding once a summer.

Since Bonnie's death, I let work and family consume me. I was fifty when she died. I guess you never get over the loss of someone you've loved almost all your life, but I did about as good as most, yet not as good as some. There were times that I thought about dating again, but I soon considered it too much work. If I was meant to be with someone, she would show up. I was convinced that that was how it would happen if it was going to happen at all. There were times that I was lonely and felt alone, but then I'd call up one of the kids and it would pass. They would keep in touch as their schedules allowed.

Then last Christmas, it all changed. While at a Christmas pageant for Simon's daughter, Alice, I ran into an old friend. Monica was now a grandmother to Joseph, one of the kids in Alice's class who was playing his namesake while Alice was playing Mary. Some might say that it was perfect typecasting. The kids were great and after the performance, we took them and their parents all out for hot chocolate and donuts.

It was remarkable how easy it was to fall into conversation with someone I hadn't kept in contact with for all those years. Monica was a widow. Her husband had died just last year during the holidays. She was feeling pretty bad, but wanted to visit his plot. I offered to take her to the cemetery the next day.

We went together in silence. I waited in the car as she walked to the niche in the Wall of Honor caring for her departed Jack. As I watched Monica obviously sobbing, I thought of my own loss and how it seemed to have been a lifetime ago since Bonnie and I had lived and loved.

I got out of the car and went to lend her support. She accepted my handkerchief and buried her head in my shoulder crying tears of pain and sorrow. She apologized and our hands touched igniting that same flame I had felt all those years ago on my sixteenth birthday. I was lost. Could this be happening all over again? Why not? Stranger things had happened. I could not bring myself to let her know of my feelings on this day, but I vowed to myself that I would soon.

For the first time since Bonnie died, Christmas this year would be a lonely one. Jackie and her family were going to Aspen to ski over the Christmas break. Simon and Mick were taking their families with them to a convention in Anaheim on the 27th, but decided to go early and take in Disneyland. They hadn't been there in years. No one had thought about me. Not that they had to, but it would be the first time since Bonnie died that I would not be with some family on Christmas.

It was Christmas Eve and I had started with the eggnog early. First it was just plain, but as it got into early afternoon, it just seemed right to add a shot of Chivas Regal to it. I watched some bowl game that didn't matter and 'It's a Wonderful Life' for the third time since Thanksgiving. Nothing helps to support my feeling of self-worth than watching that movie and trying to piece together what the world would be like if I weren't in it.

I guess I fell asleep somewhere around when Jimmy Stewart and Donna Reed (George and Mary) fell into the pool. The next think I knew the phone was ringing and ZuZu was saying, "Look, Daddy! Teacher says that every time a bell rings an angel gets its wings." The clock on the mantle said 6:25 p.m. I had slept about an hour or so.

The phone rang again. I finally got to it and answered with "Merry Christmas." Monica's voice sounded like an angel. She had been thinking about how supportive I had been the other day and wanted to ask me over for Christmas dinner with her and her son, Daniel, and his family. The fact that her only son had my name wasn't lost on me. It would be a few months later that I would find out that her grandfather's name was also Daniel and her son was really named after him, not me.

I accepted her invitation and spent a lovely Christmas day catching up on old times. Some were wonderful and others were actually boring, but not to us. As the rest of the family didn't want to hear our life stories, they went into the parlor and left us sitting over coffee at the dinner table reminiscing about the 'good old days' and wondering what might have been.

After a few hours of conversation, I got up enough courage to tell her about the feelings that stirred in me when I simply touched her hand at the cemetery. Ever since that day, I had been trying to sort out whether they were feelings for her specifically or just because she was a woman and I had been without that closeness for so long. I decided that it was Monica.

She listened, and when I finished, she reached across the table and simply put her hand on mine. Sparks flew and I could feel my heart pounding. I took her hand, stood up, and led her out onto the back porch. There we stood holding hands and looking at the moon in all of its brilliant glory. No words were spoken. I held her close. She smelled of the same jasmine perfume she used to wear when we were just kids. She melted into my arms, we kissed that same first sweet kiss, and in our own way we knew that we had come home from a journey we each had to take. We're married now and as happy as we always knew we would be.

Day Eight
The Christmas Miracle

My mother died this year. She had been unwell and, quite frankly, it was a blessing for her. She had been in and out of the hospital for the past three years, spending most of that time in convalescent homes. There wasn't one specific thing that was wrong with her. It was just a compilation of old age things. One time, it was a kidney problem, then it was high blood-pressure that was uncontrollable, and finally, pneumonia set in and claimed her lungs. She was 92 when she died.

We had been expecting her death for a few weeks. The doctors were very forthcoming about her prognosis. I let my brother and sister know of Mom's eminent death so that they could make arrangements to be with her a little while before she left to join my dad.

It took Maxie, her true name is Maxine, about four hours to drive the three hundred miles to be with Mom. Georgie had to fly in from the east coast. He wasn't even sure that he could make it because of his busy schedule, but he arranged it so that he could see his west coast clients while he was in town visiting Mom.

Maxie is a teacher in Bakersfield and Georgie is a program analyst for a prestigious consulting firm in New York City. Both of them arrived on the same day. I met them at the hospital and gave them an update on Mom's condition. It wasn't good. We made our way from the lobby up to her room and visited with her. She seemed comfortable, but wanted to talk which was difficult for her because of the pneumonia. The more we would tell her not to push herself, the more she felt that she had to tell us things.

Late in the day, we could tell that she was tired. We wanted her to get some sleep and she agreed, but before we left, she called each of us over and told us each something that she wanted us to know. She told my older brother that he had to step up and make sure that the rest of us were well taken care of. She had made Georgie the executor of her estate because he had the most business sense of the three of us. Mom had socked away a sizable amount of money in stocks, gold, and annuities. Neither Maxie nor I had any qualms about Georgie doing the right thing with Mom's estate. He had the contacts to be able to roll over the funds from the estate into a family trust. I certainly couldn't do it. What does a free-lance writer know about stocks and such?

After Georgie left Mom's bedside, Maxie leaned in and was told that she could have all of mom's jewelry. While the jewelry should have gone into the estate, my brother and I didn't want to go against Mom's wishes. Besides, there were plenty of other artifacts to go around. Dad had made a killing in real estate and made sure that Mom was well taken care of. She was an avid art collector. She and Dad also had a tremendous library of First Edition classic literature. I'm pretty sure I got my love of writing by sitting in the family library day after day reading Twain, Steinbeck, Faulkner, Crane, Poe, and many others. Georgie would probably want the art and I was pretty sure that I would be the only one interested in the books.

Finally, it was my turn to give Mom a good night kiss and hear what she had to tell me. I got as close as I could to her, kissed her on the forehead, told her that I loved her, and waited for her message. She lifted her head and simply said, "Write the story."

I couldn't think of what she was talking about so I asked her, "What story, Mom?"

Her breathing was labored, but I had to find out. She coughed a little and said, "The Christmas miracle when you were two." She coughed again and had a tough time to catch her breath. I told her that I would, kissed her again, and told her, for what would be the last time, that I loved her. It was 8:30 p.m. when the three of us left her room. We agreed to meet at 8:00 in the morning for breakfast, and went home. Unfortunately, my single bedroom apartment wasn't big enough for them so they stayed at Mom's.

It was about 3:00 a.m. when I got the call that Mom had died. I called Maxie and Georgie and told them that I would pick them up on my way to the hospital. There wasn't much that we could do, but the hospital administrators told me that they could leave Mom in her room for about an hour if we wanted to say goodbye.

It was hard seeing her so lifeless. She had been such an integral part of each of our lives as we grew up. It was sort of understood that Dad made the money and Mom took care of the house and the kids. We didn't mind it. I guess that's because we didn't know any better.

We said our goodbyes, signed the hospital's paperwork, and then left. Mom had made all her funeral arrangements in advance so all we had to do was contact May Funeral Home and let them know that we needed their services. It was too early to be in touch with them so the three of us went to breakfast.

We settled in a booth at Joy's Diner near the hospital, ordered coffee, and perused the menu. Maxie ordered eggs benedict. Georgie had his usual stack of pancakes, and I ordered ham and eggs over easy. We all drank coffee. While we were sad, it almost seemed that each of us felt a sense of relief that Mom had died peacefully and was relatively free of pain.

"Did you hear what Mom asked me to do before we left the hospital?" I asked the two of them.

Both said that they hadn't; that they were too far away to hear. "She wants me to write a story about the Christmas miracle that happened when I was two. Do you remember anything about that?" I remembered her telling me something about it when I was five or something, but it was all pretty fuzzy.

Georgie seemed to remember the most. He gave me enough that I could sort of piece it together, but it didn't seem like a 'Christmas miracle' to me. Maxie added a little more, but she was almost as fuzzy as I was. In fact, some of her information contradicted Georgie's. It would be hard piecing it all together. I guessed that all I'd do was go over the facts and write them down. I doubted that it would equal a "Christmas miracle," and certainly not any kind of story that could be published. It was probably just one of those anecdotes that gets embellished as parents keep telling the story.

As Mom was one of the most generous people in our little town, it didn't take much for the church to be packed with family, friends, and those whom she had helped along the way. She was buried next to my dad in the town's only cemetery. There was one headstone for the both of them. There was no inscription on the headstone until Mom died. Then, per her instructions, the following was added: "Jack and Nancy Robertson – Loving Parents of George, Maxine, and Robert."

Mom died during the summer and I never gave the story another thought after getting the initial information from Georgie and Maxie. Now, here it is Christmas and my conscience is getting the better of me as I ponder the events of that Christmas so many years ago. I hope that I can do it justice by piecing what my brother and sister told me along with what I remember Mom telling me over the years. My writing skill would help to fill in the gaps. Well, here goes.

It was Christmas 1950 and I was two years old. My parents weren't well-to-do then, but were generous to those in need. I suppose the three of us learned about giving from them. Dad worked at two jobs in those days to make ends meet. He was determined that my mom would not work, but stay home and take care of us kids. By then, there were three of us. I was the youngest.

I remember going out all together to find a Christmas tree for the living room. Dad insisted on a large tree. No small tree for the Robertson family. It was really, really cold in the foothills where we lived and there were patches of snow on the ground at the Christmas tree farm from an earlier storm. Mom had bundled us all in warm snow suits. With hoods and mittens on, we were kept warm. I could walk, but Mom brought my stroller just in case.

As we exited the car, both my brother and sister were let go like hounds at a fox hunt to find the perfect tree. Mom held my hand as we followed behind the 'hounds' and their hunter.

"What about this one?" Maxie squealed.

"No, this one," countered Georgie.

My brother was three years older than me and Maxie was two years older. They were very competitive and each was bound and determined to be the one to find the perfect tree for our home.

It seemed that Dad kept a tight rein on them so that they didn't get too far ahead of me and Mom. Not wanting to be outdone by my brother and sister, I started pointing at any tree that struck my fancy and yelling, "Tree, tree!"

"Yes, Bobby, those are trees," Mom would say trying to keep me quiet.

It didn't take too long before my dad and the 'hounds' were out of sight. What were we to do?

You know, the more I write this story the more I am remembering about that day so many years ago. You wouldn't think that a two-year-old would have that much memory. It must have been a significant event.

Anyway, Mom had my hand and we ambled between the clumps of trees that seemed taller than our own house. I remember thinking that we'd never get the tree through the door let alone set up in the living room. Maybe we were going to put the tree up in the front yard.

Then, all of a sudden, in the middle of the forest was a tree close to my size. I broke away from Mom and ran to it. I couldn't reach the top, but at least I could see it.

"My tree," I yelped while jumping up and down.

"That is a nice tree, Bobby. Let's see what your father thinks. Jack! Jack! We're over here. Come and see this tree," she yelled.

I don't know if she did that just to let me know that my opinion counted just as much as the other two or if she really did like the tree.

My dad showed up with Georgie and Maxie in tow.

"That's no tree. It's tiny like you," Maxie quipped.

"Yeah, we want a big tree," Georgie added.

All I could do was add my own two cents before Dad stepped in. "My tree. Tree big. My tree."

"All right, children, there's no need to fight. Bobby, I like the tree you and your mother have found, but there are a lot of trees here. Let's look a little more before we make a decision." My dad was a real diplomat.

I'm not sure that I understood all that he said, but I do remember that the tone of his voice made me trust in what he had said, whatever it was.

We spent another half hour or so looking for the perfect tree before we found it. It wasn't mine, but it was pretty nice. Dad borrowed a saw from the farm manager and cut down our perfect tree. We walked it to the entrance where Dad paid for it. It was tied on top of our station wagon by a teenage boy who I guess was working there on his Christmas break.

We all piled into the car and Maxie started to chatter with no one in particular. First it was Georgie, then Mom, and finally me.

"Who's up for hot chocolate? I love hot chocolate. It was so cold out there in the forest. Georgie, don't you want hot chocolate? Mom, how 'bout it. It will warm us all up! There's a place just down the road. Bobby wants hot chocolate. What do ya say, Dad?" Maxie chirped on and on until she got her way.

Both my mom and dad were patient people, but a bombardment by Maxie was not going to get them to say yes. In fact, it seemed to do the opposite of what Maxie wanted.

"Maxie, I'm afraid not this time. We still have a lot to do before Christmas Eve tomorrow." It was tradition in the Robertson family to decorate our Christmas tree the day before Christmas Eve.

"But, Mom, it won't take long. We can be in and out in no time. Please!" she begged.

Now Georgie jumped on the bandwagon. "Yeah, I want hot chocolate, too. Let's stop."

A chorus of 'pleases' from both of them seemed to have no effect. As we got closer to the little stand that served the hot chocolate, Maxie bent over and whispered in my ear. I listened and simply said what she told me to say like a parrot.

"Please may I have some hot chocolate? I've been good." I sounded like I was five.

Maxie was a genius. Mom turned around in the seat, looked at me, then looked at Maxie and simply said, "Yes, you have been good." Turning to my father, she said in a voice filled with emotion, "Honey, let's stop for hot chocolate."

I could see a smile on Dad's face as he turned it towards my mother. We stopped, had hot chocolate with tons of marshmallows in it, and even got to share an apple fritter with our hot chocolate.

All the way home, Mom led us in singing Christmas carols. It seemed that we were home in no time. Dad unloaded the tree and put it on the back porch until he could get the stand out of the shed. It was mid-afternoon by the time Dad got the stand and all the decorations out of the shed and into the house.

I don't know if it was the hot chocolate or the excitement of decorating the tree, but all us kids decided to play tag in the house. I guess it was fun, but I seemed to always be "it."

"Alright you three, that's enough. Go wash for dinner." Mom had been cooking an early dinner while Dad got out the Christmas things. By eating early, we could decorate the tree before we had to go to bed. Mom made our favorite mac & cheese with toasted French bread.

Maxie helped me wash my hands and face and I followed her into the dining room. My highchair was where it usually was. I could smell the spices that Mom added to the mac & cheese. It was a wonderful smell.

"Dinner! Dinner!" I shouted.

"Yes, honey. It's dinner time." Mom put me up in my chair and put the tray in front of me.

Dad came in and said, "Why is he still in that highchair? Let's put our big boy at the table with the rest of us. I'll get the booster seat. Let's see how this works."

I have always remembered how special I felt at that meal. We all sat down and started chatting. It seemed that Dad was just as excited as we were to decorate the tree. Mom brought a bowl full of the cheesy pasta to the table. She added a salad to our meal because we had to "eat healthy in this house."

I was getting impatient. How could Mom be so thoughtless as to put a huge bowl of pasta on the table so far away from me when I was clearly ready for my dinner.

"Where's mine?" I wailed.

"In just a minute, Bobby, we have to say Grace first." I didn't know what Grace was, but I knew we had to do it before eating. I quieted down and Dad led the prayer.

Mom put a large spoonful of 'dinner' in my very own bowl. I wasn't too good at eating with a fork yet, but I tried. I was having some trouble so I asked for a spoon. I decided to put less on the spoon and maybe not tip it as I brought it to my mouth. That seemed to work. Mom gave me a half slice of toast to go with my meal, but I didn't want it so I tried giving it back to her. She wouldn't take it.

"Bobby, eat all of that toast. It's good for you." I pushed it aside and made a face.

I went back to eating my pasta. It was good and so was the milk that I drank from my sippy cup to wash down the cheesy goodness.

"Who wants dessert?" Mom asked. "You have to be finished with dinner before anyone gets dessert."

Georgie frowned as he had not finished his salad. He hated salad, but liked dessert more than he hated salad so he covered the remaining bits with dressing and forced them down. Maxie never had to be told to finish her dinner. She was what parents call a "good eater." Then there was me. I had already drawn my line in the sand and refused to eat the toast I was given.

"Okay, Bobby, we're waiting for you to finish," Mom said as she pushed the toast to the center of the tray.

"No!" I said as I pushed it back to the corner.

"Bobby, no one gets dessert until you eat your toast. We're having your favorite; chocolate pudding," Mom bribed.

I don't know if it was because I was already full of chocolate from our morning outing or I was just being obstinate, but I took the toast that Mom had again pushed to the middle of the tray and threw it across the table, hitting my father right on the nose. I knew there was going to be trouble the moment I did it, so I began to cry hoping that they would feel sorry for me and not punish me for being so stupid.

I already told you that my parents were very patient and this was one of those times when Dad really had to exercise it. He simply looked at me with a blank face. He didn't seem angry or happy. His face was full of disappointment at me. I couldn't take it. Finally, I knew what I was crying for. I had disappointed my dad.

"Calm down, Bobby. It's alright. No one was hurt. You can stop crying now," Mom said with care in her voice.

My brother and sister had stopped chattering as soon as I threw the 'strike' at my father's nose. My mom's soothing voice gave them permission to speak again.

"Wow, Bobby. That was not nice," Maxie chimed in.

"I would never do that," Georgie added.

Then Dad hushed them both, took the toast that had fallen on the table, and placed it back on my tray in the center. I was still sniffling. I saw Mom look at Dad and I could tell that this incident had now become Dad's to resolve and Mom was out of it. What was I to do? I looked at my father and, without even saying a word, I began eating my toast.

Mom got up and got the pudding. I'm glad that I ate the toast. It was a way for me to say 'sorry' to my dad, but it also meant that I got to eat the best tasting chocolate pudding Mom had ever made. At least it seemed that way.

The rest of the afternoon and early evening was spent decorating the tree. Dad had a process that he would not deviate from. First, the tree was planted in the stand at exactly a 90-degree angle to the floor. After setting the tree, Dad strung the lights from bottom to top and tested them, making sure that there was not one out. The garland came next. 'Round and 'round it went, shimmering in the glow of the tree lights. The ornaments were Mom's job. As she got each one out of the box, she placed a hook on it and gave it to one of us to hang on the tree. Dad helped by lifting me up so I could decorate around the top third of the tree. My brother and sister took care of the rest of the tree. Finally, it was time for Dad to place the star on the very top. He got a little step stool and stood on the first step, stretched, and put the star where it belonged. He positioned a white light inside of the star and our tree was decorated.

Mom backed us all up to the far end of the room while Dad shut off all the lights except for the tree. It was beautiful.

"Wow!" all three of us exclaimed at the same time. It was the most beautiful tree we had ever had. I know this because I couldn't remember my one-year-old Christmas tree, so this had to be the most beautiful.

We helped Mom and Dad clean up and then we went off to bed. You know that story about St. Nick and his reindeer? I swear that I could see sugar plums dancing in my head that night. Tomorrow would be Christmas Eve and new adventures lay ahead.

The morning dawned cold and crisp. Dad had been up early, gotten wood from the side of the house, and made a fire. The house was nice and toasty.

"Mommy!" I called. She must have been outside the door because she came right in.

"Good morning. How's my little man today? Time to change you. We have a big day ahead," she said with love in her voice. I got changed with very little drama and then got dressed. I wasn't sure what this 'big day' was going to be like, but I liked the sound of it.

Mom and I went downstairs and I got to play with my toys while she made breakfast. Maxie and Georgie were already up and playing in the backyard. They were throwing a ball around with Dad. It was cold enough to see their breaths.

"Ball! My ball! Let me play!" I didn't know if it was my ball or not, but it didn't matter. I wanted to play with them.

"Sorry, Bobby, it's too cold for you to go out. Let the big kids play with your father. I need you in here to help me with breakfast. We need to eat before we go out and do our last-minute shopping. Do you want pancakes this morning?"

Silly question – pancakes are just about my favorite. "Let's cook," I said.

My mom and I cooked pancakes, bacon, and eggs. When we were finished, Mom asked me to call in the kids and Daddy. I pushed the door open and yelled, "Time to eat!" They all came running in, took off their heavy coats and scarves, washed up, and sat at the table.

Dad did that Grace thing again and we ate all that we wanted. I washed it all down with orange juice in my 'sippy' cup. I was usually clumsy with my cup, but this time I didn't spill even one drop. Mom was proud of me. It made me feel good. Little did I know that, in a little while, I wouldn't be feeling good at all.

When breakfast was over, Mom and Maxie did the dishes while I got to play some more and Georgie helped Dad bring in more firewood. With the morning chores being done, we all got dressed for one more trip to downtown for last-minute shopping. I don't know why we all had to go. It's not like any of the three of us had any money to spend.

We spent what seemed like most of the day wandering around the stores. Mom and Dad didn't seem to know what they were looking for. Even though I was being wheeled around in my stroller, I was getting tired, hungry, and I was a little wet from all the orange juice that morning. I had been doing pretty well with telling Mom when I had to tinkle, but didn't do so well when we weren't at home.

Maxie was the first to complain. "Mom, are we almost done? I wanna go home. This is boring."

Georgie added his own comments along the same line.

"Just a little while longer, honey, we're almost finished." Mom took me out of my stroller. "Bobby has been sitting for an awfully long time, why don't you and Georgie take him for a walk around the store. Don't talk to strangers and don't go outside." Those were the days when you felt okay letting a six-, four-, and two-year-old wander the store aisles by themselves. "We'll meet you near the cash register in about fifteen minutes. Do you see the big clock on the wall?"

"Yeah," replied Maxie.

"Meet us when the big hand gets on the 10. Do you understand?" Maxie and Georgie nodded their heads as an acknowledgment and the three of us wandered off on our very first adventure.

"What should we look for?" questioned Georgie.

"I don't know. How about we go back to the toy aisle and see what we may have missed," replied Maxie.

"You think that's a good idea, don't you, Bobby?" She didn't wait for a response as we took off for the toy aisle.

Just as we came down the end of the towels and things aisle, we turned to the toy aisle and there were Mom and Dad. Now this would be interesting. Maxie pushed us back away from the toy aisle and whispered, "Let's see if we can find out what they're getting us for Christmas."

I wasn't sure what that meant since I thought that Santa brought presents at Christmas. Maxie poked her head around the corner and thought that she saw Mom pick up a doll. That had to be for her.

"Let me see," Georgie quipped as he poked his own head around the corner.

It was around this time that both Maxie and Georgie forgot that I even existed. Neither of them held my hand so I decided to take a turn around the store on my own. There were so many things I could stop and see on my own without a 'handler' with me. It was wonderful! Pots and pans, glasses, dishes, all sorts of things Mom wouldn't let me touch. I actually figured out that there must be a reason that I wasn't supposed to touch these things so I didn't, but I did spend some time looking at them.

Finally, I moved down the aisle and saw the revolving door collecting and dumping shoppers with regularity. I followed one lady out thinking that I would go around and back in, but when I got out, someone took my hand and led me off down the street. I thought that it was Mom so I went along quietly. It wasn't until the lady got to her car that she noticed that I wasn't her own child. She panicked, screamed, and started to run back to the store. When she screamed, I got scared and started running myself in the opposite direction; to where I did not know. I don't know if she tried coming back for me or not. All I knew was that I should run.

I must have run a block. When I stopped, I was confused and wasn't sure of what I should do next. After all, I was only two. In some way, I still considered this an adventure so I decided to keep going down the street to see what I could see. I now know that that was not a smart thing to do. I should have stayed right where I was until Mom and Dad found me.

There were a lot of people walking on the sidewalk that afternoon. It kind of amazes me now that not one of them asked me if I was lost. Maybe I didn't look lost. I don't know. All I remember about that afternoon is that I walked and walked and walked until it started to get dark.

I had seen all that I wanted to see and decided to go back to the store, but I couldn't remember which way that was. It started getting colder and I was hungry and wet again. Where were my mom and dad?

"Mommy," I cried. "Mommy!" One lady stopped, but she was a stranger and I wasn't supposed to talk to strangers so I simply started walking again. She came after me and I ran. She was old and couldn't keep up. There weren't many people left on the streets of the little town now. It was Christmas Eve and all the stores were closed and the streets were almost deserted. Where were my mom and dad? What should I do? Well, I did what any two-year-old lost child would do. I cried.

Then I heard them, the Christmas bells. For some reason, I stopped crying and followed the sound hoping that someone was ringing the bells and could help me. I must have known that someone ringing church bells would be a safe person to help me. By the time I got to the church where the bells had been ringing, they had stopped. There was no one around, but the door was opened a crack. It was opened just enough for me to push open and go inside. It would be warmer in the church.

This is the part that Maxie and Georgie filled in for me.

Meanwhile, Mom and Dad were going crazy with worry that I was lost in the store. Maxie and Georgie couldn't remember when they had first missed me, but they were sure that there was no way I would have gone outside.

The store manager called over the loudspeaker, "Attention Anderson's shoppers and employees. Please be on the lookout for a little two-year-old boy answering to the name of Bobby. He was last seen wearing a grey snowsuit in the home furnishings department. His parents are at the head cashier's station."

After fifteen minutes, the manager decided to have his employees check all of the backrooms and loading docks. It was apparent that I was nowhere in the store.

"What are we going to do?" Mom began crying.

Dad, who always had a plan for everything, simply said, "Let's pray for guidance before we do another thing." We all held hands and said the Lord's Prayer. Then Dad said, "It's obvious that he's not in here. Let's go outside and see if we can find him out on the streets."

It was getting darker and colder. People were going home. Stores were closing. I was nowhere to be found. Dad went to a phone booth and called the police to report me missing. They were nice enough, but were short-handed on Christmas Eve. They would have their regular patrols be on the lookout for me. That's the best they could do without any suggestion of foul play being involved.

Mom, Dad, Maxie, and Georgie searched a twelve-block area, but could find no trace of me. Then it started to snow. What could be worse? They continued walking until they came upon one lonely little diner, its neon lights flashing 'open.' Dad decided to stop in to ask if anyone had seen me. No one had.

"Honey, can we feed the children? It's been a long time since this morning's pancakes," Mom said, trying to remain calm in the middle of a potential tragedy.

It was now 8:00 p.m. and the diner was just about to close, but, after hearing the story of their lost child, the owner told them he would stay opened so that they could get something to eat. He didn't even charge them. At some point in their conversation, Dad asked where the nearest church was. He wanted to go there to pray. The owner gave him directions. My dad didn't feel right not paying his bill so he left a 'tip' for the man's kindness equal to the amount of the bill next to the register.

Dad led the rest of the family to the small church. There was no one outside the church, but the door was open so they all went in. The inside was completely decorated with fresh garland, Christmas wreathes, and trees on the altar.

"Let's go up front," Maxie whispered. "I want to see the Baby Jesus."

"Baby Jesus doesn't come until later at Midnight Mass," Mom whispered back.

"Can't we go see the manger scene anyway?" Georgie asked.

"I guess we can, but just for a minute. We have to say some prayers for the safety of your brother then be on our way again to look for him," said Dad.

They all walked slowly up the main aisle to the manger scene. They were going to pray in front of it. They all knelt at the altar rail, folded their hands, closed their eyes, and Mom began with a Hail Mary. "Hail Mary full of grace, the Lord is with thee."

"Mommy?" I said as I pushed the hay away from me. I was so tired that I had gotten into the Baby Jesus' crib and fallen asleep under the hay.

"Bobby!" Mom screamed. They all got up and came to me. Dad picked me up while my brother and sister brushed me off. Mom couldn't stop crying. I even saw a tear drip down my father's cheek.

"Where have you been? Do you know how worried we've been?"

I knew they didn't expect me to answer their questions so I did what I thought would be a good answer. I hugged and kissed them.

On our way back to the car, Dad wanted to see if the diner was still open so that he could get me something to eat. When we got to where the diner should have been, it wasn't there. Well, let me clarify. The building was there, but it was closed and looked as though it had been closed for years. Dad looked inside through a very dirty window. There was dust everywhere and then he saw something that none of us could believe. He saw the money that he had left for the owner sitting on the counter still next to the cash register.

This was our Christmas miracle. Not that I was found, but that I was found with heavenly guidance.

I wasn't sure that I could piece this all together, but I think I got it right. Sixty some odd years ago, an angel of God came to my family and showed us the way. I'm betting that that same angel told my mother on her deathbed to have me write his story. Now it's written and I plan on sharing it with my family on Christmas Day.

I told them that I was writing the story and invited them all for this one Christmas. They are all coming, even the kids. It will be tight, but we'll manage. Georgie's girl, Tracy, is particularly interested as she works at a publishing house and wants to represent me if the story is any good. What do you think? Does she have an author to represent? Merry Christmas to all!

Day Nine
The Christmas Pig

It was to be a Christmas like no other. I would come away from our Christmas Eve dinner with a new appreciation for ham. Why ham, you ask? Well, let me tell you all about it.

It all started two days before Christmas. We lived on a farm in Vermont and it had been a particularly cold winter. Snow covered the ground, the road, and all the outside feed for the animals. After three days of heavy snow, we decided to put all the stock into the barn.

My little brother, Kyle, (he was four) was worried that Santa wouldn't get through because the weather was so bad. He just kept on whining all day and night. The only time he stopped was when Mom and Grandma took him into the kitchen to have him help bake cookies. Grandma baked the best Christmas sugar cookies ever. Kyle was fine until he figured out that, because of the storm, Santa would never get to eat the tasty treats.

Dad and Grandpa were off felling a tree for our Christmas celebration. They showed up around mid-afternoon with the most perfect tree ever. It didn't take long for us to move from the kitchen to the living room leaving Mom and Grandma to clean up the baking mess.

Dad put the tree in the stand while Grandpa went into the attic to search for the lights. When he found them, he took them out of the box, untangled them, laid them out, and tested each string. Miracle of miracles – they all worked! As I was now almost as tall as Dad, I got to help string the lights on the tree. Our trees were always well-lit and this year was no different.

Just as we were finishing up, Grandma brought in cookies and cocoa from the kitchen. We all took a break, enjoyed our snack, and started rummaging through the ornaments. I always liked putting the balls on the tree because Mom had a tradition of buying a special ornament for each of us every year. This year, I would be hanging twelve including the new one that read, "Eugene is keen. Merry Christmas, 1955."

Dad slipped out of the house to feed the livestock in the barn. He wasn't gone for more than a few minutes when he came rushing back in.

"Everybody, come quick! I need you," and he ran back outside. We grabbed our coats and all ran after him.

When we got outside, we stopped dead in our tracks. The snow had slowed, but the roof of the barn had caved in. All the animals we owned were in that barn. Even our Christmas turkey was fattening up in there. It didn't take long for us to find out that all the stock had been killed by the falling timbers. The stock that wasn't dead, had to be destroyed.

It really started to look as though it would be a terrible Christmas. I overheard Mom telling Dad that if it didn't stop snowing soon, she wouldn't be able to go into town to get our presents that were on lay-a-way. She also wanted to pick up another turkey for our dinner. I made the mistake of telling Kyle. He began to cry and he wouldn't stop. Mom came rushing into the bedroom where we were supposed to be playing.

"What's the matter with your brother?" she demanded. "What did you do to him?"

"Nothing, Mom. I swear. We were just talking about how we don't have a turkey or presents or anything and he started crying."

"Why did you tell him that? He's too little to understand. You should know better."

I couldn't disagree with her. As she consoled my brother I put on my coat, hat, and gloves. I wandered out into the darkening sky. It would be dinner-time soon, but I had to get out of the house for some air. I felt badly about making Kyle cry. Why couldn't I ever think before I talked?

I went behind the barn at the edge of the woods and plunged in. I just kept walking and thinking. It wasn't too long before the dark of night, the forest, and the snow storm overtook me and disoriented me. I turned around to go back to the house, but the dark changed everything. I wasn't sure where I was. The snow had covered my tracks. I thought that I was going the right way, but nothing looked familiar. After what seemed like an hour or so and no barn or house in sight, I started to worry. The snow was falling heavier now and I was getting scared, cold, and tired.

I knew that falling asleep in the snow was a bad idea, but I just couldn't help myself. Just a little cat-nap and I'd be able to go on. I stopped near some fallen logs and huddled against them to protect myself from the wind and blowing snow. As I lay between two of the bigger timbers,

I pulled the collar of my coat over my head to protect me from the cold. I was shivering. The last thing I remember was saying to myself that I'd just catch a few winks then I'd be off again trying to find the house.

I don't know how long I slept, but the next thing I knew was that it was morning and I woke up warm as toast. I should have been dead. When I got up, I noticed that the ground around where I was sleeping had no snow on it at all. Then I remembered the dream. It was fuzzy at first then became clearer. I dreamt that a pig had cuddled against me to keep me warm. Could it really have happened?

The storm had stopped and I was just about to head in the direction I thought the house would be when I heard Dad calling my name. "Eugene! Eugene! Where are you? Are you out here?"

"Dad! I'm over here. Over here!" I called back.

Dad found me and gave me a real tongue-lashing as he hugged me warm. I was used to the tongue-lashing, but the hug was something new. My dad wasn't a very emotional man.

"You scared us silly. The storm last night was the worst in years. How did you stay warm?"

I showed him the space around where I had lain all night. "Well, I did what you taught me and cuddled between two logs. I guess that kept me warm." I wasn't sure if I should tell him about the dream so I just told him about the logs.

"That was smart, but you shouldn't have gone to sleep. Good thing you stayed up most of the night. If you had fallen asleep earlier last night, we wouldn't be having this conversation."

I knew what he meant and I shivered at the thought. As we walked back to the house, I saw tracks in the snow. "Dad, didn't our pigs die in the roof cave-in?"

"Yes, all of them. Not a one survived."

I was confused. "Could there be any wild pigs out here?" I asked.

"I don't think so. Why?"

"It's just that I see these tracks that look like pigs' feet." I bent down to show him.

Dad looked at the tracks and said, "They sure do." We began to follow the tracks. They led back to the house.

I guess I had wandered farther than I thought. It took us almost two hours to get back home following the pig tracks. When we showed up in the yard, everyone came racing out of the house to greet us. Mom hugged me and Grandma kissed me on the forehead. Even Kyle was happy to see me.

"What's that terrific smell?" I asked hungry as a bear.

Grandpa came out of the kitchen. "Glad to have you back, boy. Where've you been?"

I couldn't rightly answer correctly, so I said, "I guess I've been sleepin' with the pigs."

Everyone started laughing and Grandpa said, "What are you talkin' about – sleepin' with the pigs? That's a fool thing to say."

I wasn't sure if I should tell everyone about my dream and how we followed the tracks home. They already thought I was silly, but Grandpa gave me a knowing smile.

"What's up, Grandpa? Why the big grin?"

"Well, it's just that I found a pig this morning and it's now cookin' up in the oven for our Christmas Eve feast."

My jaw dropped and I couldn't believe my ears. For all I knew, that pig had saved my life. Could I eat him for dinner?

When I got up the courage to tell Grandpa about my dream and the tracks, he said, "God provides for all his children's needs. You should be grateful for the bounty that He has provided to this family. He wants us to be happy."

I knew that he was right. When supper came, I was asked to say Grace. After a little thinking, I was able to pray, "Dear, Lord, thank you for this family, for this food, and especially for this pig that has brought us so much this Christmas." Grandpa and I both knew what I meant. From that day forward, our Christmas Eve feast would always be ham.

Day Ten
The Christmas That
Almost Wasn't

Well, here it was one week before Christmas and I was on the road with three more sales calls to make before I could start my Christmas holiday. It wouldn't be bad if these calls were in Northern California where I lived, but one was in Oregon, one in Idaho, and the other in Nevada.

Needless to say, what with travel time and the meetings themselves, it seemed like getting home for Christmas was going to be difficult. The weather wasn't going to help either. There was snow expected in all three states during the week leading up to Christmas. I had chains, but chaining up and taking them off takes time; time that I didn't have.

I called Nancy to let her know that it looked like I wouldn't make it home until the day after Christmas. She was disappointed, but knew that the three appointments could bring in enough commissions to make the house payments for six months.

It was the kids that I worried about. Janie, Mike, and Josie were all in their teens and had made it known that they wanted their father home for Christmas. They didn't quite understand how money can be more important than family. Sometimes I wonder that myself, but I still have to do what I have to do.

My schedule was tight already and there was no room to move up any of the meetings. The only thing I could do was to cancel one of them, but these were solid sales leads and the company was expecting me to close the deals with all three customers. I knew I could do it. I was not worried about that. I would figure something out. I didn't want to disappoint the kids.

"Hello, Mr. Rasmussen, please. Yes, I'll hold." I figured that it was worth a try to see if I could get in earlier for the meeting with Oregon Electric. "Mr. Rasmussen, thanks for taking my call. Here's my predicament. I have three appointments in three different states before Christmas. I'm already in Portland and I was wondering if it would be possible for us to meet this afternoon instead of tomorrow morning. That would give me a little cushion and help me get home to my family for Christmas."

"Jim, I'm glad you called. I was actually going to cancel our appointment for tomorrow due to a special board meeting. I'd still like to meet with you. Let me check my calendar for this afternoon." It took Mr. Rasmussen about five minutes to get back to me. "If you can be here in a half hour, I can give you an hour for your presentation. I've been looking forward to our meeting and I certainly don't want you to go away without us talking."

"I can make that. I'll see you at 2:30. Thanks for being so accommodating."

As soon as I hung up the phone, I left my hotel room and made my way to the meeting. It hadn't snowed yet, but the clouds were heavy and it looked like they would open up at any time. As I pulled into the parking lot, there was one car leaving that was right in front of the entrance. *A good omen,* I thought.

Twenty minutes later, I was meeting with Mr. Rasmussen. "Good to see you again, sir. How have things been going? From what I've been reading, Oregon Electric is well on its way to a good year."

"We've done alright, but I know we can do better. That's where your company comes in. We have a terrific management team here at Oregon Electric, but as the CEO of this company, I know that from time to time it's a good idea to get a pair of fresh eyes in to look at the processes and procedures. I'm looking at your company and one other to provide new insights."

"Mr. Rasmussen, you know our work and you know that we are always truthful in our analysis of procedures and processes. We at Davis, Finch, and McMahon would love to be your choice for the job."

"You know, Jim, it's not all about money with us. We want to hire someone we can trust. That's why your company is on the short list."

"I appreciate your confidence in us. We've done some preliminary work and think that we have found several spots in your organization where some savings can be made. If you give us the opportunity, we can have a team in here after the first of the year. I think you'll be pleased with what we can do for Oregon Electric."

"That sounds good, Jim, but as I said, I have one other appointment before I make my decision."

"I understand. Can you give me a timeframe for your decision-making process so that I can do some prep work should you choose our company?"

"I'll be meeting with your competitor the day after Christmas and I'll be making my decision by the Friday after Christmas."

"That sounds great. There's just one more thing. Is there anything I can do that would help you choose our company today? You have our prospectus with all that we can do and how much we will charge. Other than the appointment you have with our competitor, is there anything you hope to get from them that we haven't offered?" I wasn't sure about this strategy, but if I've learned anything in my life as a salesman, it's to always be closing.

"Jim, I appreciate your desire to land our company for your company, but I'm a man of my word and I need to meet with the other company before I make up my mind. I hope you understand."

He looked a little annoyed.

"Of course. I appreciate you making the time to meet with me today. I hope that you and your family have a Merry Christmas and Happy New Year."

As I got up to go, Mr. Rasmussen got up from behind his desk, came around, and extended his hand. "I'll give you a call the Friday after Christmas with my decision. Have a safe trip to your other appointments and Merry Christmas to you and your family."

So the meeting didn't go as I had planned. I'm a pretty good closer, but I just couldn't close the deal that day. I did feel good about the meeting, though. *Next Friday will tell the tale.*

As I exited Oregon Electric, those clouds that were holding so much snow were dropping their load onto Portland. I went back to my hotel, went to dinner in the hotel restaurant, and went back to my room to prepare for my next customer in Idaho. Before going to bed, I called Nancy.

"Hi, Babe, it's me. How was your day?"

"Oh, you know. The same old thing the week before Christmas; shopping, decorating, and partying. What time is your meeting tomorrow with Oregon Electric?"

"Well, I got lucky and was able to move the meeting up to this afternoon. Couldn't close the guy, but we're on their short list. He'll be making a decision next Friday after Christmas. I feel pretty good about this one."

"So, what about the other two? Do you think that you can get in early with them? The kids would love for you to be home for Christmas. So would I." She had that seductive tone in her voice that she uses whenever she wants me to really do something.

"I'll be leaving for Idaho tomorrow morning if I can get out with the snow that's falling. Once I get there, I'll see if I can get an earlier appointment. I'll do the same for Nevada when I get there. How are the kids?"

"They're fine. They've done a great job helping me with the decorations and wrapping. They're out bowling with their friends right now. Mike and his friends hung up the Christmas lights. I knew you wouldn't have time. They did a good job."

"Well, if all goes the way I'm planning, I could be home on Christmas Eve. Do you have any plans for either Christmas Eve or Christmas Day?"

"We're having our Christmas Eve open house and then going to your parents for dinner on Christmas. Pretty usual stuff."

"What did you get the kids for Christmas? Anything with 'some assembly required' this year?"

She laughed. "They're older now so toys aren't really what they want. I got them some clothes and a gift card to their favorite store. Kids like to spend money that's not theirs."

"That sounds good. Guess I'll get some shuteye so I can get started early tomorrow. It's snowing here, but hopefully, it will be clear tomorrow for my ride to Idaho. I'll call you tomorrow night. Good night. I love you. Say hi to the kids for me."

"Good night. I love you, too."

As luck would have it, I was able to get earlier appointments and close both of the deals in Idaho and Nevada. I was now on my way home. The weather wasn't too bad, but I had to be careful with the ice on the road. Tomorrow would be Christmas Eve and I was looking forward to being with Nancy and the kids.

Just as I was leaving Las Vegas, a snow squall hit and I had to pull off to the side of the road to be safe. I stayed there for about three hours before I started up again. By the time I got to Bakersfield, I was ready for a nap so I stopped at a motel and crashed. I didn't wake up until 9:00 a.m. I checked out of the room, grabbed some pancakes at the local IHOP, and got gassed up. I should be able to make it all the way to Sacramento on one tank. I thought I'd better call Nancy to let her know what was going on.

She didn't answer her phone so I left her a voicemail message. "Hi, Honey. Just letting you know that I had some trouble with the weather out of Vegas and had to stop in Bakersfield overnight. I'm leaving now and should be home around 4:00. Love you."

The drive home was uneventful and I pulled into the driveway about 4:15.

I walked into the house to the smell of my favorite meal, spaghetti and meatballs. Nancy was at the stove and the girls were setting the table.

"Hey! What's for dinner?"

"Dad!" both girls yelled as they ran over to hug me and kiss me welcome home.

"Glad you made it for the party. All of the family is coming over," Nancy said.

"What party?" I teased. I walked over to Nancy and gave her a peck on the back of her neck.

"Dad, you made it home. That's great," said Mike. "What do you think of the lights?"

I hadn't really noticed, but told him that they looked great.

"Okay, let's eat," Nancy called. The kids like mom's spaghetti as much as I and they didn't need to be called twice for their favorite meal.

We all ate our fill. The kids cleared the table and put the dishes in the dishwasher. Nancy and I went into the living room, looked at the tree, and cuddled on the couch. Mike came in and lit a fire in the fireplace.

"Thanks, son. You're getting to be a handy man to have around the house."

"Aw, Dad. I'm going to my room until the families show up."

The girls went to the back room to watch some TV.

"Looks like it's gonna be a great Christmas. What did you get me?" I pried.

"I'm not going to tell you. What fun would that be when you open your present," Nancy responded. I laughed.

The families came over. We ate, drank, sang songs, exchanged some gifts, and went to bed around midnight. The next morning, we all got up, got dressed, and made our way to the 9:00 Mass. Besides the Mass, there was a concert by the choir. I love that choir mostly because my sister and brother both sing in it.

After Mass, we went home and I cooked my famous Christmas morning blueberry pancakes with bacon, juice, and coffee or cocoa.

"Everybody get enough? I'm stuffed. Let's clear the table and go open our presents," I said.

Every year, I select one of the kids to play Santa and distribute the gifts. They have to wear a Santa hat and give out all the gifts before anyone can open anything.

"Mike, will you play Santa this year? You've done a great job while I was away."

"Hey! What about us?" the girls shouted in unison.

"You'll get your turn next year."

Mike gave out all the gifts, we all opened them, and bagged all the trash for the girls to take outside to the trash can.

"Dad, you make Christmas fun. I'm so glad that you made it home," said Mike.

"Ditto for me," said Janie and Josie.

Nancy came to me, wrapped her arms around my neck, and simply said, "Merry Christmas, Santa," then looked up at the mistletoe and gave me a kiss.

By the way, I got the contract at Oregon Electric.

Day Eleven
The Family Christmas Secret

Christmas Eve 1940 is a Christmas I will never forget. It started out like any other season. November brought cold winds and snow flurries to Western Maine. My brothers and I had to hike to school in the snow. Our parents didn't believe in 'snow days' and neither did our teacher. Our one-room schoolhouse was about a mile away and we walked it every day because my dad had to use the truck for hauling logs from the forest to Frenchville.

We lived about two miles outside of town and walked everywhere. Even in 1940, Frenchville was a tiny community. The population today is still under 1,000. It was originally founded as a trading post in 1783 near the mouth of the Madawaska River by the two Pierres; Lizotte and Duperre. It was incorporated as a city in 1869, but was still very small.

So, here I am at age 75 going to tell the story that I've held inside for 60 Christmases. I guess I've never shared it because it is too fantastic. Some might call it unbelievable, but it happened. Now, at 75 and in ill health, I don't care if people believe me or not. I just don't want to die without my story being told. Believe it or not, it's true and I'm going to tell it as best as I can remember it.

My name's Jake Bradford and the story I'm going to tell happened when I was fifteen. It was Christmas Eve, 1940, and Mom was worried about my father. He left early in the morning to deliver wood so that he could be back early to put up the Christmas tree with the family. It was now 3:00 p.m. and the sky was filling up with clouds. Through the static of our radio came Christmas carols with the sporadic news report. The NBC mid-afternoon news announced that we would have a white Christmas with a major storm coming down from Canada.

Without saying a word, I knew what my mom was thinking. "Someone may have seen him in town, Mom. I'll go check. I can get there and back before the storm hits." I started putting on my boots, jacket, and gloves.

"You're not going anywhere. I need you here. What if your father doesn't get back in time? Who will take care of the animals? You know that your brothers don't know how to do that. They're too young."

It was true. My 6-year-old twin brothers could barely take care of themselves. Mom had a point, but what about my father? I took off my outer wear and settled in to wait for my dad to get home. I decided to make myself useful and set the tree in the stand so we could decorate it when he got home.

It would have been so much less stressful if we had a telephone. We could have called into Jim's General Store to see if anyone had seen my dad. We could have called the police to see if there were any reports of accidents. We could have called the hospitals in Frenchville and St.

Agatha to see if he had been admitted. There were a lot of things that we could have done if we had a telephone. I made it a point to make sure we got one.

An hour later, I went back to my mother. "Mom, there's still time for me to get to town and back before the storm hits and it gets too dark. Let me go. I'll be back before you know it."

"I am worried, but I don't want to have to worry about you as well," my mom said.

"The cows have been milked and they don't need to be fed until I get back. What do ya say, Mom?" I started putting on my boots, coat, and gloves again. This time, I put on a toke to keep my head warm.

"If you promise to come back as soon as you find anything out, I guess it will be alright. Try and find a ride back if you can."

"I will, Mom." I kissed her on the cheek, ran out the door, and down the path leading to the road. I had already figured that I would hitch my way into town and save some time that way, but it all depended on what traffic there was. I didn't know what to expect on Christmas Eve.

The snow crunched under my feet as I made my way to Jim's General Store. I could see my breath; it was that cold. The clouds were thick with snow. I prayed that the storm would hold off. The forest along the path in the St. John's Valley was as quiet as a vacant chapel except for the breeze blowing through the tree tops, causing a flurry now and then as the snow fell from the trees. I liked that because it was so spontaneous. I never knew when one was coming. The moon was full and it lit my path through the clouds. I didn't even need a lantern.

It only took me about a half hour to get to Jim's. As I got there, Jim was just closing up.

"Jim," I called from up the road. "Wait up. I need to talk to you."

Jim turned from locking the door to the general store. "Why, Jake, what are you doing out here on Christmas Eve? You already bought your Christmas presents."

I jogged the rest of the way to the porch of the store. "Have you seen my father? He was supposed to be home early this afternoon. He had only a few wood deliveries on the other side of town, but we haven't seen him all day."

"I haven't seen him at all," Jim said as he put the keys in his pocket. "How can I help?"

Jim was a long-time family friend and was used to extending our family credit when we couldn't pay for the necessities of life. My dad always made sure he got paid in full with a little extra for his kindness.

"I was wondering if I could use your phone to check with the police and local hospitals," I said in a strained voice.

"Sure, come on in. I'll get the numbers." He unlocked the door and turned on the lights.

I called all the numbers and no one had seen him, but the police took down the information on my dad's truck and were going to keep an eye out for it. I guessed that that was all that could be done so I asked Jim for a ride back to the house.

"Sure, kid. Get the lights, would you?" Jim went out first and when I shut the lights off, I noticed that there was a light on in the back room.

"I'm going to shut that light off in the back," I shouted to Jim.

"No! It's okay. I leave it on so that people think someone's working late. Don't go back there. It's fine."

This was the first time I had ever seen Jim agitated. Why was he agitated about a light on in the back room?

"Okay, hop in. I want to get home before the storm hits," he said.

"So do I. I really appreciate this." We never spoke all the way home. Something was wrong. I didn't know quite what. All I knew was that Jim was acting fidgety ever since I noticed that light in the back room.

"You can let me off here," I told him at the foot of our pathway to the house.

"I'm sure that your dad will be just fine. Don't worry about him. I'll see you the next time you come to town. Merry Christmas!"

He made a u-turn and headed back to town. I thought that was odd since his house was a few miles up the road. I don't know what came over me, but I had a wild urge to see what was in that backroom. I started jogging back to the store.

When I got there, Jim's car was parked. I figured that he was just going in to shut off the light. I went around back to see what I could see. Light dripped out of the icy window panes, but there was not much to see. Just then, a full moon slipped out from behind the clouds to light up the whole night with its reflection off the snow.

I couldn't believe my eyes. There in the trees was my dad's truck. What was Jim up to? Could it be that he didn't know that my dad parked his truck back there? What could be going on? I decided to put my ear to the window and see if I could hear anything. What I heard was muffled, but I could just barely make it out. It was my dad and Jim in a heated conversation.

"Jack, I told you that this would be dangerous and that we shouldn't have any part in it. What are you going to do now? Your kid was up here asking about you. He even called the cops and the hospitals! Don't you think you should go home?" Jim said with some urgency in his voice.

"Look, Jim. We started this together and now we're into it up to our necks. There's no way out except to do what we said we'd do. I have to protect my family and you have to protect your business."

"I know, I know, but why do we have to do it on Christmas Eve?"

"You know as well as I that the client needs his delivery tonight. Let's quit all this jawwin' and get the truck loaded so we can get home."

"Alright! Alright!" Both Dad and Jim headed for the back door. I sprinted for the trees to see if I could figure out what they were up to.

Dad got in the truck and moved it down to the back of the building. Both he and Jim loaded about twelve boxes of something in the back of the truck. Dad covered it with a tarp and tied it down. They both got into the truck and Dad put it in gear and headed for the road.

I don't know what came over me, but I ran to the back of the truck and, while Dad checked for traffic, I untied one corner and snuck under the tarp into the back of the truck. I expected to find moonshine or some other illegal substance, but what I found floored me. There in the bed of my dad's truck were twelve boxes of dynamite. I was scared. What if he hit a bump or a rut? Were these things safe? All I wanted was out of that truck.

About a half hour later, the truck slowed down and stopped. I was trapped. How was I going to explain this? I decided to try and get out the same way I got in and hope that neither of them would see me. No such luck.

"Jake! What are you doing here?" my dad yelled at me. "You can't be here. It's too dangerous."

"Tell me about it. Is it more dangerous than taking a ride with twelve boxes of dynamite in the back of your truck? What's going on, Dad?" I was really upset and didn't mind showing it.

"Jack, we have a job to do. Take care of your domestic issues later. C'mon. We're gonna be late," Jim said as he picked up two of the boxes.

"Alright, just give me a minute. Jake, I'll tell you all about it later, but now I have to finish this delivery or I'm in big trouble. Do you understand? Now go get in the truck and wait for me."

I headed toward the passenger side then turned around. "Do you need any help? As long as I'm here, I can help unload and then we can get out of here. What do you say?"

My dad looked at me and said, "I guess you can help, but be careful. We need to go to that cabin through the trees. Just take them to the break in the trees just in front of the porch. Do not go into that cabin. I don't want you to know who we are dealing with." I did as I was told.

After my second load, I made my way back to the truck. As I approached it, I heard some rustling in the trees. I thought that it was a coon or a squirrel, but I was surprised to see men with guns drawn. It was Mack Wilkins, the County Sheriff.

He put his finger to his lips and simply said, "Shhh!" I didn't make a sound even though I wanted to warn Dad and Jim. The Sheriff pointed at one of his men to stay with me. That's just what he did. No conversation or handcuffs or anything. He just stood there with his gun drawn.

In a few minutes, I heard shouting. "Get your hands up! County Sheriff Wilkins here. You're all under arrest for receiving stolen property."

I heard my dad and Jim plead their case and I also heard two other voices that I knew. It was Parson Everett and his son, William. When it was all over, I was in cuffs as were all of the others. We went to the County jail to be booked. I was in the same car with my dad.

"Not a word, Jake. I'll tell you all about this when we get out of jail." I wasn't sure how Dad knew that we would be getting out of jail, but I went along with his request because I was just a little scared.

When we got to the jail, Sheriff Wilkins un-cuffed Jim, me, and my dad. "I thought that there was only going to be two of you on this sting?" questioned the Sheriff.

"Yeah, so did we," quipped Jim.

"Anyway, you did good work tonight. I don't know what those guys had planned for this shipment of dynamite that we intercepted, but I'm pretty sure that it wasn't going to be to blow up tree stumps. I'll have your reward money in my office by next Thursday. Remember, not a word of this to anyone. We may need you again. Thanks."

"You're welcome and don't worry. We won't say anything even though I'm pretty sure that we won't be doing this again," my dad said.

"I'm with you on that, Jack," added Jim.

Sheriff Wilkins looked at me and asked, "What about you, young man? You can keep this to yourself, can't you?"

I didn't have to even think about it. "I sure can, Sheriff. You can trust me on that."

With that, the Sheriff shook all of our hands, tipped his hat, and made his way back into his office.

Dad just looked at me as we headed back to the truck. "I'll ride in the back," I said as it began to snow.

We dropped Jim off back at the General Store and I got in the front. After a few minutes, I couldn't hold back any longer, "Well, what was the deal?"

"Do you really want to know? I mean, the less you know the less you have to keep secret."

He was right, so I didn't probe for more information. "How are we going to explain this to Mom?"

"Well, I had that all planned until you came along. Now I have to think up something new."

"Why? What was your story? Maybe we can still use it or parts of it," I said.

"I was going to use two flat tires as a reason for not getting back early, but now I have to worry about you."

"Why is that? You can say that you ran into me on the way home and picked me up. I can go with that story. It's not exactly a lie either. You did pick me up at the General Store even if you didn't know it. What do you say? Is it a story?"

I could tell that Dad was thinking. "I guess it will do. I hated making your mother worry, but the money was good and I helped get some bad guys that we trusted in this community off the street."

"I'm proud of you, Dad. Now let's get home and trim that tree."

"You got it, son."

When we got home, I let Dad do all the talking. He's a pretty good storyteller. Mom believed every word, served up dinner, and we all trimmed the tree.

Even though I was only fifteen that Christmas, I felt as though I became a man because my dad, the Sheriff, and Jim trusted me with the secret. They're all gone now and I'll soon join them, but I wanted the world to know how my dad, the owner of Jim's General Store, and I helped to foil a major theft ring.

There, it feels good to get that off my chest. I'll be reading this story to my grandkids and great-grandkids at Christmas dinner tonight. I wonder if they'll believe it. It doesn't matter. How about you? Merry Christmas!

Day Twelve
The Secret of Christmas Valley

"I'm a Pulitzer Prize winner for crying out loud! Why are you giving me this fluff piece only three days before Christmas?" I was angry that my editor passed over some up-and-coming reporters to give me the Christmas lead for Christmas Day.

"What about Roberts?" I bellowed as I shut the boss's door. "Don't you think that he'd jump at the opportunity for a byline? Just explain to me why you think that this is a good idea?" I held my tongue for the first time since Joe Clark, editor of the Daily Journal, told me about the assignment.

"Are you finished?" he asked. "Because, if you are, I'll explain it to you, even though I don't really have to. Are you ready to listen?" He paused and waited to see if I was interested in his answer or not. I was, so I just kept quiet and sat down in the chair opposite of Joe's desk.

"All right then. I've selected you for this assignment specifically because you are a Pulitzer Prize winner." He had my interest.

"Tell me more," I said quietly.

"It seems that there is a small town in upstate Vermont that believes that they are all employees of Santa Claus. It's a small town of about 856 people and each of the adults and some of the older kids work at the only manufacturing plant in town. Do you want to guess what they manufacture?" He paused waiting for me to bite.

"I don't know, toys?" was my silly answer.

"You're right. What I'm about to tell you came directly from a citizen of the town. Why is this so surprising, you're thinking? Well, it's because no one ever leaves Christmas Valley, Vermont, or so I'm told."

"Hold on a minute. So far, all you've told me is a fantasy with some sort of rebel spilling the beans about this town, Christmas Valley. Have you looked it up on the internet or in the State records?" I was becoming angry again. "What due diligence did Clark do before deciding that this was an 'explosive' story that just had to have me as its reporter?"

"Of course, I have!" Now Joe was getting angry. "Do you honestly believe that I'd give you a story if there was no merit to it? I thought you trusted me more than that."

"Alright, alright, I apologize. Tell me what you found out." I decided to give him a chance to finish the story before I would comment further.

"So, this Jim O'Rourke from Christmas Valley was having a drink down at Shaughnessy's on High Street. It just so happened that Jackie Michaels from the Fashion Section was in there to interview Lila Cambridge, the fashion designer. Lila always holds interviews in bars. She calls it free advertising. Anyway, Jackie overheard this O'Rourke fella chatting with the bartender."

"Was she that close to him that she could overhear a personal conversation? Are you sure that Jackie didn't make up this whole thing?" There, I'd done it again – show my mistrust for another employee.

"So, do you want to listen or do you want me to throw you to the dogs to dig up all your own information?" He looked me straight in the eye.

"Sorry, Joe. Go ahead," I responded.

"Jackie and Lila were sitting in a booth right behind O'Rourke who was at the bar talking with the bartender. According to Jackie, he seemed pretty distraught about something. At first, she kept on hearing him say, 'I shouldn't have done it' over and over again."

Now my interest was piqued. "What is it that he shouldn't have done? Is he a fugitive or something?"

"No, nothing like that. It ends up that he was sad because he left Christmas Valley. He said that he was the first to leave in almost fifty years. He was afraid of what his leaving would mean to the town."

"Starting to sound like a silly story again, Joe. What difference could one man leaving a small town make? Just sounds like regret for leaving, but nothing more. So, where's the story?" I was getting a little perturbed that it was taking so long to get to the point.

"This is the story. After having a few drinks too many, O'Rourke told the bartender that his leaving could cause the whole town to disappear the day before Christmas leaving Santa with no toys for all the kids in the U.S."

I was speechless, not because I believed it, but just the opposite. I deal in facts not fairy tales. The only thing to be found in this story, if there really was a story, was that this O'Rourke had a wild imagination tied to Christmas.

"And you believe this fantasy story? I thought you were more in tune with reality than this, Joe. You really want me to chase down a story about a disappearing village that will take away all the toys for kids in the U.S. because Santa won't be able to stop at his U.S. plant to stock up for his flight around the country? Do you see how unbelievable and silly that sounds?" I paused, waiting for Joe's response.

Joe got out of his chair and came to the front of the desk. I got up to meet him. "Tim, do you trust me? I mean really trust me?"

I had to think about that for a second, but Joe had never led me wrong before, so I simply said, "Yes."

"Then, trust me when I say that I know there is a story here bigger than what we know now. I can't tell you how I know. I just do and I want you to uncover what's really going on in Christmas Valley because I trust that you won't fall for the first explanation one of those local yokels will give you. Can I count on you doing your best on this?"

I had never seen Joe so passionate about a story that, on the face of it, seemed to be nothing. "Alright, Joe. I actually had no plans for Christmas anyway. I might as well work. What's the deadline for this?"

"I need to have a draft in my hands by noon on Christmas Eve. If it's everything I think it is, it will be the lead on Christmas Day. That gives you about two and a half days to get the story, draft it, and get it to me. I know that it's a tight deadline, but I know you can do it."

I was already starting to have second thoughts about the assignment. My first thought was to find this O'Rourke and get more information, but then I thought of the time I would waste if I couldn't find him right away.

My next thought was to get up to the top of the state and check out this Christmas Valley. Just as I was leaving the building, I thought I'd pop into Fashion and see if Jackie could give me any more information.

I was in luck; she was sitting at her desk banging out her next day's fashion tips.

"Jackie," I interrupted. "How have you been?" I didn't wait for her to answer. There was no time. "Joe Clark just told me an amazing story about a conversation you overheard at Shaughnessy's. Can you tell me what you know? I've been given the Christmas lead assignment and I'd like to find out more."

"Well, Tim, I'm fine. Thanks for asking," she said sarcastically.

What was the matter with me? I knew better than to treat my peers like they didn't matter to me. Just because I had the Pulitzer was no reason to be short with other reporters no matter what their beat was. "I'm sorry, Jackie. I should have let you answer before I started off on my 'quest for the truth.'" I used my fingers on each hand to quote that last part.

"I get it, Tim. Take a seat," she said as she pointed to the chair right next to her tidy desk.

I don't know what I expected, but a desk with little out of place told me something about this Jackie Michaels. I was right. As she filled in the details of the overheard conversation, it was obvious to me that Jackie was every bit the reporter that I was.

"Did you ever hear where O'Rourke was staying here in Londonderry?" It was just an off the cuff question that I didn't expect an answer to, but Jackie responded immediately.

"He's staying at the Londonderry Arms, room 232 and before you ask, I went up to the bar after my interview with Lila and sat close enough so I could hear more of the conversation. Once, while he was pulling out some cash to pay for his last drinks, he put his room key on the bar practically in front of me. It was almost as though he was inviting me to join him. We never spoke, but I chatted up the bartender after O'Rourke left."

"What did he have to say?"

"Well, nothing at first. Seems that his mouth only works when his palm has been greased with cash. I gave him all I had for a ten-minute conversation. He made $20 and I had a fantastic story that truly was fantastic."

"So, if it was so fantastic, why did you think that Joe would want to have someone follow-up?" I asked.

"I really don't know. Call it intuition or simply the desire to maybe prove this O'Rourke wrong. It could be either one. Anyway, I gave Joe the story and expected that that would be the end of it. But, now here you are. Guess it wasn't so fantastic after all."

I rubbed my chin in thought and gazed into Jackie's soft blue eyes. "Do you believe this story, this O'Rourke?"

She thought for a moment. "I do," was simply all she said.

"What are you doing for the next few days?" I respected Jackie Michaels and thought that two of us working on this piece could finish it off sooner and get us home earlier for Christmas Eve. Little did I know the danger I was asking Jackie to share with me.

"I actually just finished my last piece for the year. I have a week's vacation starting today. What did you have in mind?" she seemed interested.

"How would you like to share a byline with me on the Christmas lead? You know as much as I do about Mike O'Rourke, Christmas Valley, and this disappearing act that may happen if he doesn't go back. What do you say? Are you in?" I was hoping for a quick response because "time was a wastin'."

All she said was, "Let me get my coat. Do we have time to stop by my place to pick up a few things?" I hadn't even thought about that.

"Sure. We'll stop by your place then swing over to mine. The drive to Christmas Valley should only take a few hours. If we're lucky, we can wrap this up in a day or two."

The two of us left just as though we had been working together for years. The drive up was interesting. I learned more about Jackie and she learned more about me. It was interesting that our paths to the jobs we currently held were similar. We both worked on the school paper in high school, earned a Journalism Degree in college and came out looking to change the world with our insightful reporting. We both languished with papers in some backwater towns until we got a break and moved up to the city. My Pulitzer was a surprise. I never wrote with the intention of winning any kind of award, but my month-long expose on crime in small town America got me noticed and, as the weeks passed, more and more people read what I was writing. The more I wrote, the more people sought me out to tell me their story.

By the end of the piece, I had exposed several small-time crooks that were arrested and put behind bars for various offenses like loan sharking, money laundering, and fraud, just to name a few. To tell you the truth, I was glad when the piece was finalized. The more I dug the more corruption I was finding. Finally, I turned over everything I had to the DA except the names of my contacts. They took it, ran with it, and helped to clean up the city.

Christmas Valley sat at about 3,500 feet elevation and, while it didn't always get snow, it was snowing today. Luckily, I had snow tires on the car. The snow wasn't very deep, but better safe than sorry.

It was almost 2:30 pm when we rolled into town. Main Street was decorated for Christmas just as you'd expect for this time of year. The shops were small and seemed to be busy. As we would find out later, there was no mall in Christmas Valley so the local merchants were able to keep their businesses opened without the competition of a Big-Box store.

"What do you say we get something to eat before we find a place to stay? I'm famished," Jackie said.

"Sounds like a plan. Let me know if you see a place to stop." It only took a few minutes to drive down Main Street and it seemed that there was only one diner in the entire town. I made a U-turn and found one of the diagonal parking spots right in front of *Mama's Good Eats Diner*. We got out of the car, trying not to slip on the snow that was beginning to pile up on the street as well as the sidewalk.

As we walked into the diner, it was like entering another world. There were Christmas trees and wreaths all over the place. There was even an electric train running above the dining area. There were dolls and stuffed animals everywhere. Each little table was decorated in green and red with a candle for ambience. We stopped at the sign that said, *Please Wait to be Seated.* We didn't have to wait too long before a woman dressed as Mrs. Claus ushered us to a table near the back of the diner, gave us menus, and told us that our server would be with us shortly.

"Strange place, huh?" I said.

"I guess you could say that, but maybe not so strange if you consider the name of the town – Christmas Valley," Jackie analyzed.

"I guess you're right." I opened up the menu and, for whatever reason, I was surprised to see plain American food. I guess I expected to see some exotic meals that would go with Christmas. The only thing I saw that remotely looked like a Christmas meal was the special of the day, shepherd's pie. My dad used to make his version of that English delicacy every Christmas. He said that it reminded him of his mother's meat pie.

"What are you going to have?" I asked Jackie. "I'm going to have the shepherd's pie."

"That sounds good, but I think I'll just do Mama's Cheeseburger."

It wasn't too long before our server, Jeanette, came by to take our order. The meal was great and Jeanette did a nice job of serving us. I left her a nice tip. I'm generous that way. Service people work hard for the precious little they get so I try and help whenever I can. Jackie noticed my generosity and asked if she could pay half of the bill.

"No need. The paper will be picking up our expenses. It will just be easier if I present one bill instead of two." After I said that, I started wondering if the paper would pick up any of Jackie's expenses since she was really on vacation and with me because she was interested in the story instead of being assigned to work on the story. No matter.

By the time we finished our meal, it was around 3:30 and starting to get dark with the cloud cover. "We'd better find a place to stay before it gets really dark out," Jackie stated. We called Jeanette over to see where the local hotel or motel might be since we never saw one as we perused Main Street.

"There is no hotel or motel within fifty miles of here. You can stop at the end of the street and ask Mama if she has any more rooms to let. She owns the large Victorian on the hill." I gave Jeanette a larger tip for the information and scribbled a note in my expense pad.

I wasn't sure what Jackie was thinking, but I was wondering what we would do if there was only one room available. We parked at the bottom of the short climb that took us to the front door of *Mama's Boarding House*. Jackie rang the bell and we waited.

The door opened just a crack, "Yes, what can I do for you?" asked a little old lady that just let her head peak out the door. Her voice was raspy and reminded me of my own grandmother.

"We were told by Jeanette at the diner that you may have a room or rooms available for a day or two. I have cash and am willing to pay in advance." The old lady relaxed a little and opened the door so that we could enter. At least that's what we thought.

"What's your business here? There aren't many that just come up here for the mountain air or the sights."

She caught us off-guard, but Jackie was quick on the up-take. "My husband and I work in the city and like to get away every once in a while to recharge our batteries so to speak. We are just looking for some place to simply relax and enjoy the season."

The old lady looked us up and down and decided she liked what she saw. "Well, I do have one room, but you were asking about one or two rooms. What kind of relaxing were you going to do with two rooms?"

I answered that before Jackie got us into more hot water. "That was just a slip of the tongue. When I travel on business, I usually have an assistant with me and we always have separate rooms."

Mama accepted that explanation, nodded her head, and moved aside to let us in. "Do you have any luggage?" she asked.

"Yes, we do. I'll get it after we sign in and check out the room if that's okay."

"That'll be fine, sonny. A body can't be too careful. People without luggage tend to up and leave in the middle of the night. Now, you said that you could pay cash up front, is that right?"

"Yes, ma'am. How much for the night? I'm not sure if we'll need a second night or not." She looked up at me with a quizzical look in her eyes.

"Thought you said you wanted to get up here to relax and yet you're already thinkin' about leaving tomorrow. What's that all about?"

The old bird was cagey so I had to be cagier. "I'm sorry, you misunderstood. We plan on staying the two nights and I'll pay you for the two nights, but we never know what may come up from home. We have two kids staying with Grandma and Grandpa for the first time."

"I see. That makes more sense to me. Here, just sign the register. I can give you room three at the top of the stairs. It's the best room in the house. It overlooks the entire downtown area. That'll be $80 for both nights."

I was a little confused. "You mean $80 per night, right?" I questioned.

"No, son. It's $40 per night to stay at *Mama's*. Breakfast will be from 8:00–9:00 am. Tomorrow, we'll be having French toast, bacon, juice, coffee, and fresh fruit. I may also have some yogurt available. You folks enjoy your stay in Christmas Valley." She turned and left the parlor without even checking any ID or making sure that we signed the register.

"She's a strange old lady," Jackie chortled. She kept giggling as we went to get our luggage.

"So, Mrs. Wright, what do you propose we do about our one bed situation?"

Jackie smiled and said, "That's easy. I get the bed and you get the floor."

How did I know that was coming? Oh, well, a few nights on the floor won't hurt – much.

Since we had eaten a late lunch, we decided to stroll around town and see what information we could dig up. After three hours of 'shopping' for information, it became clear that there were secrets in Christmas Valley. Secrets that most were either unaware of or unwilling to divulge. We got back to *Mama's* around 8:00 pm. When we opened the door, the smell of freshly baked cookies and cocoa filled the room. There on the coffee table in the center of the parlor was a plate of crunchy chocolate chip cookies and a pot of chocolate. I love my cookies to be crunchy and so did Jackie, I found out.

"These are great!" Jackie exclaimed. "I wonder where the other guests are."

That was a pretty good question. Mama was nowhere to be found so we just ate our cookies, drank our chocolate, and talked about our strategy for the next day. We decided to try and visit the toy manufacturing plant on the edge of town. It would prove to be more trouble to get in than we had imagined.

The night was uneventful. She had the bed and I'm sure she was very comfortable. I found the floor a lot harder than I thought it would be. The combination of the floor and her snoring kept me up most of the night. Since I was up anyway, I used the time to take my laptop into the bathroom and begin writing what I hoped would be the story Joe Clark wanted.

By 8:30 we had both showered and gotten dressed. As we opened the door, the smell of sizzling bacon and coffee quickened our step and let us virtually fly down the staircase to the breakfast table. The table was beautifully set with a crème Chantilly lace table cloth, green and red woven napkins, and highly polished silverware. On the sideboard were hot pans with the breakfast that was promised – French toast, bacon, eggs, and a bowl of freshly cut fruit of the season.

As we were both hungry, we ate our fill and then some. We washed down our breakfast with cups of steaming hot coffee. It wasn't until we had finished breakfast that we realized that there were no other guests at breakfast and Mama had not joined us. We finally figured out that there probably were no other guests and that Mama was busy elsewhere on the property. The breakfast was too good to go unrewarded, so I left a $10 bill on the corner of the table.

It didn't take us long to find the plant. We parked in the Visitor's Stall and made our way to the gated entry.

"May I help you?" the diminutive guard asked.

"Hi, I'm Tim Wright and this is my wife, Jackie." I thought that we might as well maintain the same cover. "We are visiting in town and thought that we'd like to see how toys are made. Do you have a tour that we could take?" That would be too easy and I expected a no, but got something completely different.

"Sure, there are no other visitors today, but I think that I can get someone to give you a tour. Please follow me."

As soon as the guard left his post, another showed up to take his place.

"Can you wait here for a moment? It won't be too long," the guard said.

"What are you thinking, Jackie?"

She thought carefully before she spoke. "That was almost too easy. What do you think we'll find on this tour?"

"I was thinking the same thing. I don't know what we'll find, but it's a good place to start. Maybe we can find someone in here that's willing to talk to us about the secret."

Just then a man who looked a lot like Santa came out of the upstairs office, walked down the stairs, and introduced himself to us. "Hi, I'm John Peterson and I'll be your guide today." He extended his hand in friendship.

"Hi, John. Pleased to meet you. What's with the Santa outfit? I mean, I know that this is a toy factory in Christmas Valley, but it seems a little over the top to have a guy dressed as Santa running plant tours." I was a little shocked at my own boldness in approaching the question that way.

"Okay, you caught me. I'm not really John Peterson and you're not really on a tour of the plant. Follow me, please."

What had just happened? One minute we were going to take a tour and now we're not. "Wait a minute! We're not going with you anywhere until you tell us what's going on. So, if you're not John Peterson, who are you?" I was afraid that I knew the answer already and I was right.

"I'm Santa Claus and this is my U.S. workshop. Please, follow me. All will be made known to you in a very few minutes." Santa walked off down the shop floor.

Jackie looked at me and just shrugged, "Well, we came here for a story. Let's see where this leads us."

She was right, of course. While I was busy getting all balled up in who or what the man in the red suit was, Jackie kept her eye on the object of our visit – to learn things. We followed Santa, if that's who he really was. He led us up the stairs to a smallish conference room.

"Can I get you anything to eat or drink? I have hot cocoa, crunchy chocolate-chip cookies, or just plain water."

I wasn't sure where this was going, but I supposed that a snack couldn't hurt. We both opted for the cookies, but Jackie asked for a glass of milk instead of the water or cocoa.

"Of course we have ice cold milk. How silly of me not to offer it. Mrs. Claus will be right in, then we will have a little talk." Santa left and almost immediately, as though she heard us ordering, Mama from the Room and Board showed up and delivered our snacks.

"Mama? What are you doing here?" Jackie asked in surprise.

"Well, I'm pretty sure that young Timmy here has figured out that Mama is really Mrs. Claus. Isn't that right, Tim?" She turned her head from Jackie and looked me straight in the eyes.

"It didn't take a genius to figure it out. Santa said that Mrs. Claus would be bringing in the snacks. Can you tell us what Santa wants to talk to us about?" I was hopeful that I'd get some advance information, but none was forthcoming.

"You'd better wait for Santa. He's in quite a predicament and needs your help," she said disappearing into the next room.

We had just enough time to finish our snack when Santa came back into the room with Mama. He pulled up a chair and sat right in front of us. "So, here it is kids – the reason that you were sent to Christmas Valley. I was only expecting one of you, but I think we can make it work with the both of you. Don't you think so, Mama?"

"Of course we can, Santa, but please tell them why they are here."

We were both on pins and needles to find out, when Santa began the explanation. "You see, kids, this manufacturing plant is really one of my many workshops around the world. All of the toys for every good little boy and girl on the Nice List is made here. On Christmas Eve, I make a stop here right after my trip through Canada, pick up all the toys, and make my U.S. run. I am only able to collect the toys if everyone in Christmas Valley is sound asleep in their beds. That has never been a problem before, but this year, there will be one bed empty."

"Let me guess, Mike O'Rourke will be absent, causing you to miss your U.S. run. Is that about the gist of it?"

"That's exactly the gist of it. Mike needs to come back, be in his bed, and sound asleep before midnight on December 24th or I'll have to move on without any delivery."

Jackie asked an obvious question. "Why do all the people need to be asleep and how do you know if they are or not?"

"It's simple, Jackie. Everyone in this town has been programmed since birth to be in bed by midnight. They've been told that the town would disappear if they weren't in their beds at midnight. When midnight rolls around, I recite the words of the Christmas spell that puts everyone asleep for a period of a half hour. That gives me just enough time to load the sleigh and take off for my U.S. run. By putting everyone to sleep, I'm assured that no one will see me take off. This workshop is the secret. To some, it's a toy manufacturing plant, but to my elves who run the plant, Mrs. Claus and I, this is the U.S. toy workshop that provides all the toys to the U.S. on Christmas Eve and Christmas morning."

While this Santa spun a good yarn, I wasn't quite ready to buy into the whole thing just yet. "So, what is it that you want us to do?"

Santa wiped his mustache and proceeded to tell us that I was selected by Joe Clark to help track down Mike O'Rourke and bring him back up to Christmas Valley. He also told us that Joe used to live in Christmas Valley, but left during the fleeing time. Each year between 1 June and 31 August, all citizens have the right to come and go as they please, but, if they are not back by August 31st, it is determined that they are no longer a resident of Christmas Valley and, as such, cannot stop Santa from making his run.

Santa poured himself a cup of cocoa and continued with his story. "You see, Mike O'Rourke left during December and needs to be in his bed by midnight or the repercussions will be grave for all the U.S. children. Joe thought that if anyone could find Mikey O'Rourke, it would be you. The bonus was that Jackie overheard Mike's conversation."

"What luck that I stopped in to chat with her before I left. But how can I find him if I'm up here. I need to get back down to Londonderry and find him. We know where he was two days ago and maybe he's still there. But, how am I going to get him back up here? Does he know what's at stake if he doesn't come with me?"

Santa sat there with his head in his hands. "That's the challenge. Mike lost his wife to cancer two years ago and his little girl was killed by a hit and run driver while riding her bike in the street. Mike hasn't been the same since. He is determined that no child will have a Merry Christmas because of his circumstances. It's sad, I know, but you have to convince him to come home just for this one night. I wish I could simply ignore his absence, but I can't. The only way I get off the ground with toys is if everyone is in their beds fast asleep."

I looked at Santa, then to Mrs. Claus, and finally to Jackie. "I really don't know what to do here. I'm not a psychologist. How can I take a man from his grief in just two days and convince him to do the right thing? Santa, this is impossible. Can't you find a work-around for just this one year?" I was starting to panic.

"There is no work-around. There is only you."

"And me," piped in Jackie. "I think I know how to help. My minor in college was psychology and I had an opportunity to work in a clinic with a fantastic doctor for a semester. I'm not saying that I'm a doctor, but I really enjoyed the class and the internship. I feel pretty confident that I can open Mike's mind to the idea of returning for the others even if it won't be for his daughter."

While Jackie had good intentions, I wasn't sure that we should trust this to her after one semester of an internship. "Jackie, are you still in contact with this doctor and do you think that he'd help us?" I asked.

"Sorry, he's out of the country for Christmas. I got a Christmas card from him a few days ago. He won't be back until the new year."

"Well, it looks like Jackie will have to do," said Santa.

Jackie actually looked as though she relished the opportunity to get into Mike's head. "Come here, child," said Mrs. Claus. She gave Jackie a hug and whispered something in her ear.

"We'd better get going," said Jackie. "Let's not stop to get our things. We can get them when we come back with Mike," Jackie said.

Without another word between us we were off. Something had changed in Jackie. I was noticing a whole new person. She had changed from someone content to stay in the background and let me do all the talking to now being a person in charge. I wondered where she got this new-found self-confidence.

As we drove into Londonderry, Jackie directed me right to the hotel where Mike had been staying. With any luck he would still be there. We took the elevator to the second floor and went to his room. I knocked twice and waited for a response.

"Who's there?" Mike yelled through the door.

I wasn't prepared to answer that question, but Jackie was. She put her mouth to the door and in a very quiet voice said that she had a message from Mrs. Claus for him. I wasn't sure that he had even heard her.

I knocked on the door again. "Mike, can we come in for just a minute. It's important."

The next thing I heard was the door latch being opened. He simply said, "You can come in now," as he backed away from the door.

Jackie took the lead as I thought she should. "Hi, Mike. How are you feeling? Have you had anything to eat today? We can help you with that if you want." She was so good at putting him at ease.

"Well, I am hungry. Can you get me a burger from the corner diner?"

I don't know if he was testing us or not, but Jackie knew just what to do. "Sure, we can do that," she said. "Do you want to go out or would you rather that we get it and bring it back to you?" She was smooth.

"I think that I'd like to have it brought in if you don't mind."

"No problem at all. What would you like on it?" Mike gave Jackie what he needed to have a great burger. "How about some French fries? Do you want those or chips? How about a soda?" She was doing a good job at keeping his mind occupied.

"Do you mind if Tim and I eat with you? It's been a long day for us as well."

She had done a masterful job in providing him the opportunity to feel that he was in charge. "Sure, get whatever you want," Mike said.

"Okay, so that's three burgers with the works, two with fries and one bag of chips along with three sodas – make mine a diet." She turned to me and asked, "Do you need any money?"

I said no, and got the drift. She wanted to be alone with him. I didn't know what she had up her sleeve, but after what I had just witnessed, it was obvious that she could handle him by herself. I left to get the food and ran all the way to the diner. Why, I don't know.

When I got back, Jackie and Mike were in the middle of something funny, because they were both laughing up a storm. "What did I miss?" I asked.

"Oh, nothing. Did you get everything?" she asked.

"Everything and more. They had these little homemade apple pies so I got us each one."

"That sounds great!" exclaimed Mike. "Let's eat. I'm starving."

We each grabbed a bag and tore into the food. It was almost a race to see who could devour their burger first. Truthfully, they weren't that good, but it was what helped to open the door to Mike's subconscious. At least that's what I thought. Jackie would tell me the truth sometime later.

"Wow! I'm stuffed," said Jackie. "How about we save those apple pies for the trip back to Christmas Valley?"

I was looking at Mike to see what his response would be. It was not what I expected.

"Good idea. Let me just pack up and we can be on our way," he said.

I was surprised and wanted to help so I asked, "Do you need to pay your bill for the room? I can get that while you're packing if you want."

"No, it's fine. I paid it while you were out. I'll only be a minute more then we can head on out."

While he went into the bathroom to collect his toiletries, I pulled Jackie aside and asked her what happened to make him so eager to get back to Christmas Valley. She said that it was complicated and that she'd tell me after we delivered him to his home in Christmas Valley.

The drive back seemed to take forever. Jackie and Mike seemed to have hit it off really well. They chatted the entire way back while I drove.

"Okay, we're here. Where do you live?" I asked.

"Just take me to *Mama's*," he replied.

I wasn't sure what this was all about, but Jackie seemed fine with it. As soon as I parked the car, Mike jumped out of the car and ran up the walkway, the stairs leading to the door, and went inside yelling "Mama!"

"What's with him?" I asked.

She just looked at me with tears in her eyes. "He's home."

I looked at her in disbelief. "You mean that he's their son?" How crazy could this story get? She just nodded.

I took Mike's bag up to the parlor where I could hear happy voices chattering in the kitchen. It looked as though Santa would be making his U.S. run after all.

It had been a long day, but Jackie and I decided to get our things and head back to Londonderry. We still had a story to write, but what would that look like? We got home around 10:30 pm and agreed to meet for breakfast at the diner around the corner from the paper. I was on time and she was late.

"What kept you? I almost left. So, do you have any idea for a story that we can tell that won't blow our readers' minds? I'm stone-cold blocked. I've started three different angles on this, but am getting nowhere. What do you have?"

"What can I get you to drink this morning?" asked our server.

"Two coffees. Make them strong and keep them coming. We have a long day ahead of us."

Well, we finally did find an angle about the Christmas spirit that permeates Christmas Valley. The boss wasn't thrilled, but he knew what the real mission was and was happy that we had accomplished it.

Just as we were getting ready to leave for the Christmas holiday, I had just one final question to ask Jackie. "What was it that Mrs. Claus whispered in your ear just before we left to get Mike?"

"Ah, I was wondering when you would get around to asking me that. That's the secret of Christmas Valley and I'm not allowed to share it with anybody."

"Fine, be that way. What are you doing for Christmas dinner tomorrow?"

She paused, looked me square in the eyes, and simply said in her husky voice, "I thought you'd never ask."